PIRATTITUDE!

So You Wanna Be a Pirate?

Here's How!

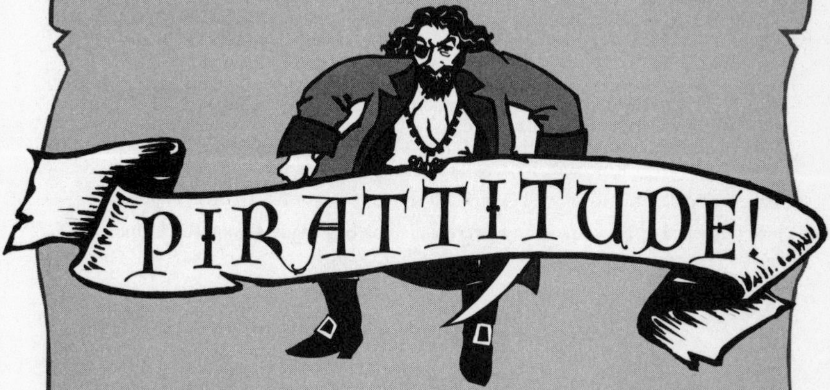

PIRATTITUDE!

So You Wanna Be a Pirate? Here's How!

JOHN "OL' CHUMBUCKET" BAUR

and

MARK "CAP'N SLAPPY" SUMMERS

NEW AMERICAN LIBRARY

New American Library
Published by New American Library, a division of
Penguin Group (USA) Inc., 375 Hudson Street,
New York, New York 10014, USA
Penguin Group (Canada), 90 Eglinton Avenue East, Suite 700, Toronto,
Ontario M4P 2Y3, Canada (a division of Pearson Penguin Canada Inc.)
Penguin Books Ltd., 80 Strand, London WC2R 0RL, England
Penguin Ireland, 25 St. Stephen's Green, Dublin 2,
Ireland (a division of Penguin Books Ltd.)
Penguin Group (Australia), 250 Camberwell Road, Camberwell, Victoria 3124,
Australia (a division of Pearson Australia Group Pty. Ltd.)
Penguin Books India Pvt. Ltd., 11 Community Centre, Panchsheel Park,
New Delhi - 110 017, India
Penguin Group (NZ), cnr Airborne and Rosedale Roads, Albany,
Auckland 1310, New Zealand (a division of Pearson New Zealand Ltd.)
Penguin Books (South Africa) (Pty.) Ltd., 24 Sturdee Avenue,
Rosebank, Johannesburg 2196, South Africa

Penguin Books Ltd., Registered Offices: 80 Strand, London WC2R 0RL, England

First published by New American Library, a division of Penguin Group (USA) Inc.

First Printing, September 2005

10 9 8 7 6

THE LIBRARY OF CONGRESS CATALOGING-IN-PUBLICATION INFORMATION:

Baur, John.
Pirattitude! : So you wanna be a pirate? : Here's how! / John "Ol' Chumbucket" Baur and Mark "Cap'n Slappy" Summers.
p. cm.
Includes bibliographical references.
ISBN 0-451-21649-0
1. Pirates—Humor. I. Summers, Mark. II. Title.
PN6231.P53B38 2005
818'.60708—dc22

2005007785

Printed in the United States of America

To Charlie Summers,

Ed Baur,

and Tom Summers,

three sailors who helped show us the way

Contents

Foreword

Arrr! I was both surprised and delighted to be asked to write the foreword for this very funny book. Delighted because, while I've never sailed with Cap'n Slappy or Ol' Chumbucket (no matter what they claim) I am familiar with their work and admire their effort to spread the joy of pirattitude.

But I was also surprised because, after all, I've been dead since 1718 and just don't get out much anymore.

Life on a pirate ship isn't all broadsides, beatings and boardings. There's barnacle scraping, deck swabbing, knot tying and lots of other tedious nautical stuff to do. If you're a captain and want to stay a captain, you have to make sure that there's time for fun.

In these pages, Cap'n Slappy and Ol' Chumbucket have captured the fun side of being a pirate. They've got the swagger and the growl down pat. It's funny stuff the lads have come up with, and no mistake.

Buccaneering is a serious business, and the pirate's life can be a hard one. So let me just say I hope you enjoy this book as much as

I did (one of the perks of writing the foreword is I got a sneak peak at the galley proofs) and remember to talk like a pirate every September 19.

Edward "Blackbeard" Teach

Introduction: Plundered from Dave Barry

The following is taken from the writing of syndicated columnist Dave Barry, winner of the Pulitzer Prize and our close personal friend, although in the name of complete candor we have to admit that we've barely met him. The column appeared Sunday, September 8, 2002.

Every now and then, some visionary individuals come along with a concept that is so original and so revolutionary that your immediate reaction is: "Those individuals should be on medication."

Today I want to tell you about two such people, John Baur and Mark Summers, who have come up with a concept that is going to make you kick yourself for not thinking of it first: Talk Like a Pirate Day. As the name suggests, this is a day on which everybody would talk like a pirate. Is that a great idea, or what? There are so many practical benefits that I can't even begin to list them all.

Baur and Summers came up with this idea a few years ago. They were playing racquetball, and, as so often happens, they began talking like pirates. And then it struck them: Why not have a day when EVERYBODY talks like a pirate? They decided that the logical day would be September 19, because that—as you are no doubt aware—is Summers' ex-wife's birthday.

Since then, Baur and Summers have made a near-superhuman effort to promote Talk Like a Pirate Day. As Baur puts it: "We've talked like pirates, and encouraged our several friends to, every September 19, except for a couple where we forgot."

And yet, incredibly, despite this well-orchestrated campaign, the nation has turned a deaf shoulder to Talk Like a Pirate Day. In desperation, Baur and Summers turned to me for help. As an influential newspaper columnist, I have the power to "make or break" a national day. You may recall that almost nobody celebrated Thanksgiving until I began writing about it in the 1970s.

I have given Baur's and Summers' idea serious thought, looking for ways to improve it. One variation I considered was Talk Like a Member of the Lollipop Guild Day, on which everybody would talk like the three Munchkins in the film version of *The Wizard of Oz* who welcome Dorothy to Munchkinland by singing with one corner of their mouths drooping down, as though they have large invisible dental suction devices hanging from their lips. But I realized that would be stupid.

So I have decided to throw my full support behind Talk Like a Pirate Day, to be observed this September 19. To help promote this important cause, I have decided to seek the endorsement of famous celebrities, and I am pleased to report that, as of today, Tom Cruise, Julia Roberts, Britney Spears, Brad Pitt, Oprah Winfrey, the Osbournes, Tiger Woods, Ted Koppel, the Sopranos, Puff Doody and the late Elvis Presley are all people who I hope will read this column and become big supporters. I see no need to recruit President Bush, because he already talks like a pirate . . .

Talking like a pirate will infuse your everyday conversations with romance and danger. So join the movement! On September 19, do not answer the phone with "Hello." Answer the phone with "Ahoy, me hearty!" If the caller objects that he is not a hearty, inform him that he is a scurvy dog (or, if the caller is female, a scurvy female dog) who will be walking the plank off the poop deck and winding up in Davy Jones' locker, sleeping with the fishes. No, wait, that would be Talk Like a Pirate in *The Godfather* Day, which is another variation I considered ("I'm gonna make him an offer that will shiver his timbers").

But the point is, this is a great idea, and you, me bucko, should be part of it. Join us on September 19. You HAVE the buckles, darn it: Don't be afraid to swash them! Let's make this into a grass-roots movement that sweeps the nation, like campaign-finance reform, or Krispy Kreme doughnuts. I truly think this idea could bring us, as a nation, closer together.

But not TOO much closer. Some of us will have swords.

1

The Lure of the Sea

(or a Reasonable Facsimile Thereof)

Can ye smell it? Aye, 'tis the smell of salt sea air, tar, wood and sweat. Ye can hear it, too: The bendin' o' the mast, the wind beatin' ragged sails and the crash o' breakers against a creaking hull create a symphony o' sounds that tug the hearts of a chosen few.

"Chosen?" ye ask. Aye. Chosen by Neptune to live and die upon the sea as

if it were yer birthright. To be a man or woman of adventure and courage; to be truly ALIVE, to know what fear tastes like and to swallow it—sharp pointy bits and all—this is what it is to have pirattitude.

Aboveboard— All honest and on the up-and-up, with nothing hidden. Trading ships would hide illegal cargo deep in the hold belowdecks. Anything that was legal would be kept out in the open, above the board, where anyone could see it. It was like saying, "Hey, come steal our legal stuff! It's all aboveboard!"

Whether you really live a life of the sea or simply get your fun imagining you're striding the rolling quarterdeck of a tall wooden sailing ship, you are probably one of the lucky people whose life is ruled by pirattitude.

"But what," you ask breathlessly, because you're the kind of person who asks things breathlessly, "what is this mystical quality you call pirattitude? And more importantly, how do I get it?"

Lucky for you, you seem to have asked the question while holding this book, because in the following pages we will answer all your questions and then some.

Remember when you were a kid (unless you currently *are* a kid, in which case that makes no sense, but you get the point) and you misbehaved in some way, acting like the rapscallion we know you can be? And when your parents called you on it, you gave them what you thought was a clever answer but they called it "sass"? At that moment, your mother probably looked at you and said, "Don't you give me any of your attitude!" Well, pirattitude is just like that—only with a pirate on top. And having a pirate on top can get you into just all kinds of trouble, especially if you're a grown-up with a responsible job and a spouse and kids or things like that. Banks get nervous making home loans to people who say, "Arrr! Scupper me if the missus and I haven't taken a likin' to that colonial on Maple Street, don't ya know."

Which is, of course, the whole point. Pirattitude is the swagger in your walk, the growl in your voice, the wicked gleam in your eye as you make your way through life. You're harming no one, but no one is going to harm you, either.

And if the loan officer doesn't like it, you've got a plank for 'im! You'll get the money someplace else, possibly a Spanish galleon.

Now, there may be some who say, "You can't teach pirattitude. You're either born with it, or you're not." To this we emphatically say, "Nonsense!" and give the naysayer a savage beating with our fists and foreheads. Because you, too, can have pirattitude, even if you never come closer to a life at sea than watching Jacques Cousteau on old *National Geographic* specials. If we didn't believe this with all our hearts and souls, why would we be writing this book and counting on you to buy it?

In the pages that follow, we'll take you on a whimsical journey o' revolutionary freedom. When we're done, you won't recognize yourself.

And we mean that in a good way.

Who Are the Pirate Guys?

We are now the Pirate Guys, but in the beginning we started out as Mark Summers and John Baur, two guys who, by a combination of accident, chutzpah and sheer dumb luck, created International Talk Like a Pirate Day, the one day a year

Edward Teach
Nickname: Blackbeard
Turn-ons: Random violence, the stench of hell, rum!
Turnoffs: Kittens, daisies, pop music
Favorite weapons: His six pistols
Ship: *Queen Anne's Revenge*
Head: Left hanging from the bowsprit of his conqueror
The most notorious pirate of them all. He was well over six feet tall, with a maniacal light in his eyes and fearsome strength. Teach got his name from his imposing beard into which he tied fuses, which he lit when going into combat for that extra, "Ohmigod, I'm fighting the devil himself!" effect. Blackbeard was known for his cruelty, not just to his victims but to his own crew. He once fired his pistol randomly under the table while dining with crew members, just to see what would happen. In his short career he terrorized the coast of the American colonies. Blackbeard was tracked down and killed by a party led by Lieutenant Robert Maynard on November 22, 1718, a subject he's still touchy about.

when people are not only allowed to talk like pirates, but actually encouraged to. Here's how we did it. Not why—since we're not sure ourselves—but how.

Aft— The rear of the ship, or more generally the rear of anything or anyone. A pirate describing overtaking a prey might say something like, "She tried to turn tail, but we took her from the aft and boarded." It has a much different connotation today, doesn't it?

There was a time when we thought we could get ourselves "back into shape," as if we ever were in shape in the first place. So we found ourselves on a racquetball court at the local YMCA, sweating and grunting as we flailed away ineffectually at a bouncing blue ball. A shot caromed just out of reach and one of us—there's no telling who, now—reached too far. Something was strained that was best left unstrained and the person let out a cry of anguish—"Arrr!" We immediately began insulting each other in pirate lingo.

Armed to the teeth— Going into combat, a pirate wanted to be armed with as many weapons as he could conveniently carry. Cutlass in hand; several pistols (each was only good for one shot) tucked into various sashes, belts and boot tops; a knife or twelve hidden on his person and even one clenched in his teeth. When you go out to cruise for members of your favorite sex, you want to have your pickup lines all ready. This way you are armed to the teeth with sexually witty repartee.

When the game was over, we realized we had had more fun than ever before on the court and the time had passed more quickly than usual. We decided, right then and there, to create a new holiday. And that was how International Talk Like a Pirate Day was born. We picked September 19 because it was Mark's ex-wife's birthday. The date was stuck in his head and he wasn't using it anymore.

For the record, she's okay with it, once she understood that we weren't being mean. We just needed a date we'd be able to recall. In fact, she now says she's never been so proud to be his ex-wife. That's what we call a good sport!

And that's where things stood for seven years, and they might have remained there if we hadn't somehow mysteriously come to the attention of

Pulitzer Prize–winning humorist Dave Barry. (Okay, we admit it. We sent him an e-mail. Nothing mysterious about it.) To our surprise, he wrote a column about the holiday and the rest is, if not quite history, at least a good story. Anyway, we now consider Dave (we call him Dave) our close personal friend. We don't think he'll mind, as long as no one tells him.

As a result of that fateful encounter at the Y (and we are saddened to report that our hometown Y has not yet put up a plaque memorializing the historic event) and our e-mail to Dave, we became the Pirate Guys. We've taken on pirate personas—Mark is Cap'n Slappy and John is Ol' Chumbucket. And our holiday went around the world faster than Francis Drake—the legendary sea dog and privateer took almost three years to circumnavigate the globe. Talk Like a Pirate Day was celebrated in Australia two weeks after Dave's column appeared. Of course, they were talking that way two weeks *before* the column appeared as well. Australians ALWAYS talk like that. But the point is, they were aware of the holiday.

Millions of people have "p-arrr-ticipated" on all seven continents—yes, even Antarctica, where a research station near the pole made a point of being our southernmost celebrants. They were joined by Boy Scouts in Malmo, Sweden, a private school in Sierra Leone, a boating club in Japan, and lots more people everywhere.

Barnacle— A crustacean that attaches itself to rocks and the hulls of ships. Calling a person a barnacle is a sign of respect, or even manly affection. "You old barnacle," you might say, lauding him for his crustiness and ability to rip the shit out of an unsuspecting beachcomber's trousers.

Belay— Shut up! Specifically, "belay" means to tie off a line. "Belay that line!" the captain might shout. In a broader sense, it means stop what you're doing, and this is where it fits most neatly into pirate lingo. "Belay that talk," you'd yell at your friend as he's about to blurt out to your girlfriend what you did last night with the twin cocktail waitresses.

And Why Pirates?

Pirates were the bad guys, right? We certainly thought so, and have said so prominently on our Web site, www.talklikeapirate.com. We wanted people to understand it was the attitude of the buccaneers we were encouraging, not the actions. "It's TALK Like a Pirate Day," we'd say over and over, "not Commit Felonies Like a Pirate Day."

Of course, that clear statement—"Pirates are bad"—brought dozens of letters arguing the fact.

Look, we don't want to debate it. Maybe pirates were misunderstood. Maybe they were, as our angry correspondents claim, an early democracy, the first stirrings of the common man uniting against the aristocracy, or an inevitable proletarian reaction to the rise of capitalism. Maybe they were bloodthirsty cutthroats. Or maybe they were just ethically challenged merchant sailors.

That's not the point.

Pirates were cool. That's the point. The buccaneers of the sixteenth through eighteenth centuries were, as one historian puts it, "the freest people on earth." And it's that freedom, that swagger, which appeals to people today.

Talking like a pirate is fun. And it's our goal to share that fun with you, whether you're an old sea dog or a hopeless landlubber. By the time you're done with this book, you'll swagger like Blackbeard himself.

A word of warning, though: Since this is all about having fun, we decided against the laborious, time-consuming research process of looking stuff up. Instead we opted for our tried-and-true process of pulling stuff out of the air. (That's the polite way of saying it. We've been accused of pulling our "facts" from a less atmospheric location also beginning with the letter A. 'Nuff said.) Oddly, we seem to be right more often than not. At least, we've gotten surprisingly few rebukes for getting things wrong. All we can guess is that "pirate-ese" is one of those things you just pick up, almost by osmosis, as you're growing up.

Still, that's no guarantee that most of what you're going to read is even close to the truth. Our research methods mostly involved beer and pizza. But remember, we don't really care. So by all

The Birth of Pirattitude

The concept of pirattitude has been around for centuries. The word "pirattitude" was coined during a radio interview in the summer of 2003. John and Mark were being interviewed on KZEL-FM in Eugene, Oregon. The interview was proceeding much as the previous dozen or so had when Mark had a brainstorm, catching John by surprise.

"How difficult is it to learn how to talk like a pirate?" DJ Kevin Kirk asked.

"It's fairly easy once you have pirattitude, and then you just kind of play it from there," Mark said. In the background of the taped interview, you can hear John laugh so hard in surprise that he actually shot coffee out his nose.

Belaying pin— Did you ever watch a pirate movie and notice that in hand-to-hand combat, they were often swinging these short wooden clubs at each other? They (the clubs, not the pirates) seem to be posted all over the railings of the ship, and are the perfect objects for sneaking up behind someone and whacking him in the head. For years we wondered, "Why did these ships keep racks full of cudgels along the railing, providing anyone sneaking aboard with a handy weapon?" Turns out these are belaying pins, stout wooden dowels that fit into holes, usually along the railing, that are used to tie (or "belay") ropes. Instead of tediously untying the knot, you just have to pull the pin and the line is free. One suspects, watching the movies, that if everybody pulled all the belaying pins for a fight, before they could start swinging, the sails would come plummeting down from the masts and cover everyone on deck.

means, keep score at home! Keep an exact tally of exactly how many things we got right and how many we got wrong. It'll be fun!

But keep it to yourself.

Sporting Insults

As you've learned, or perhaps already knew, International Talk Like a Pirate Day got its start on a racquetball court, where your heroes played gamely, if ineptly, and hurled piratical insults at each other. But what, you may wonder, did they actually say? Here's a list of things a pirate guy can yell at an opponent.

Arrr! Ye slapped that one off me mizzenmast, ye blighter!

Watch as I fire this shot straight up yer poop deck!

This ought to plug yer bunghole!

Taste my steel, pasty boy! (Technically the racquet is more likely to be aluminum or graphite, but just try shouting "Taste my graphite" and see how it sounds.)

Another shot like that and ye'll dance the hempen jig!

Come around for another broadside!

What If . . .

There are those, believe it or not, who wish fervently that we hadn't lapsed into pirate patois during our racquetball game, leading to the creation of International Talk Like a Pirate Day. Imagine what ideas for an international holiday we might have come up with if we hadn't. Now aren't you naysayers glad we did?

Slapshot Saturday
The Village People Appreciation Day
The World Festival of Groin Injuries
The Blue Ball Bacchanalia
September 19 Sweat Soirée
The Goober Pyle Experience (Reenactments of *Mayberry R.F.D.* episodes)
Dermatological Anomalies Day
National Day of Bellyachin'

QUICK QUIZ

1. Pirattitude is to attitude as:
   a) hemlock is to lock
   b) deodorant is to odor
   c) pie-eyed is to pie
   d) teenagers are to grounded
2. Racquetball is a good cardiovascular workout because:
   a) it gets you moving and keeps you moving
   b) of all the shouting and swearing
   c) you constantly have to walk around the court to pick up the balls you missed
   d) of the windmill effect of missing shots
3. True or false: Pulitzer Prize–winning humorist Dave Barry is likely to seek an injunction against the Pirate Guys if they don't quit

Blow me down— A sailor with good sea legs could stand up in the strongest gale. If something COULD blow him down, that would be quite surprising. So this is a phrase to be used when you receive really surprising news. ("Your ex-wife called and said she decided it was all her fault so she's giving back all the money." Your reply is, "Well, blow me down!") But remember that it obviously has another connotation in this day and age, and that gives it great comic potential.

claiming he's their close, personal friend. How about Cap'n Slappy's ex-wife? Is she likely to take legal action against them? If so, what's their best defense?

4. Some historians say pirates were bad people. Others say they were misunderstood. Would it be fun to lock all those historians in a room until they came to an agreement? What if you had to be in the room with them? Would you provide airholes? Why or why not?
5. The Pirate Guys say their research involved more beer and pizza than actually looking stuff up. What toppings do you think they ordered and why?

2

Pirattitude: Getting in Touch with the Pirate Inside YOU!

In Which the aspiring pirate learns whether he or she has the right stuff down deep inside.

Boarders— Pretty much every pirate movie has a scene in which the pirates, with knives clenched in their teeth, swarm to the deck of their opponents' vessel. They are boarders. When you swing into a bar or a party at someone's house, you could be one, too. Be sure to call out, "Boarders away," or something similar as you make your entrance. Conversely, if you are hosting a party and unwanted crashers show up, cry out, "Prepare to repel boarders!" Of course, this too has a sexual connotation. Cap'n Slappy's pungent odor would repel even the most enthusiastic of attempted boarders.

So now you know what pirattitude is. But how do you know if you've got it?

Recently at a Pirate Encounter therapy session, Dr. Phil Buttinski spoke at great length about the human need to "get in touch with the pirate within."

"The reason we're locking you in the room for the next three days without food or water," he continued, "is to help you conjure your inner pirate self and take control of your own destiny."

Moments later, the group of four men and seven women, all of them insurance agents from Cleveland, Ohio, beat the doctor senseless with their fists and foreheads, took his keys and money and went on a savage rampage of the Sheraton Inn. The buffet luncheon for the Daughters of the American Revolution did not survive.

What Dr. Buttinski gave those people was a sense of their own pirattitude. And in true pirate form, they never paid him.

To truly understand your level of pirattitude, we need to take a walk into the dark recesses of your imagination. To do this, we have devised a brief "Finish the Story" scenario for you. We will assess your answers and tell you whether or not you have true pirattitude.

Marvin works for your typical company in your typical office setting. He is called up to his boss's office. "Marvin," the boss begins, "I think we need to discuss your paperwork. You're two months behind and we here at—" Suddenly Marvin:

a) commences weeping, apologizing and begging the boss not to fire him

b) leans back, lights a cigar and says, "You can have

genius or you can have paperwork. You can't have both. Now, get out of my office and get to work."

Evaluation point #1

If you answered (b) you may well be on your way to claiming pirattitude. If you answered (a) we have some work to do. Let's start by recognizing that there is a freedom in being completely screwed. Your pay stinks. Your job stinks. Your spouse is cheating on you. Your children despise you. Each month places you deeper in debt and the only glimmer of hope in your pitiful life is that the same month that makes you poorer also brings you thirty days closer to the merciful release of inevitable death. See? You're completely screwed. You have nothing to lose. Your boss won't be expecting it when you go back and choose (b). Remember: He can kill you, but he can't eat you. Now, let's pick up the story:

Marvin's stunned boss gets up, collects his meager personal belongings and begins to leave. "Where will I work now?" A kindly, generous smile crosses Marvin's face. "Oh, by all means, take my old cubicle."

"Thank you," his former boss says as he stumbles out the door. Marvin puts his feet on the desk and breathes in the cigar smoke. Soon the phone rings. It's the chief financial officer. She is gorgeous but has a reputation for crushing the testicles—real and metaphorical—of any male she believes to be weak and tedious. She says, "I want you in my office ten minutes ago—where the hell are you?" Marvin takes another drag off the cigar. Then he:

Long John Silver
Status: Fictional
Rating: Classic character
Vehicle: *Treasure Island*, book and movies
There have been several portrayals of this rogue, but our favorite would have to be Robert Newton's from the 1950 Disney version of *Treasure Island*. Newton is often credited with creating the common perception of what pirates sound like. Wallace Beery was also good in the part in the superior 1934 version of the story. And while we're on the subject, let's agree right here and now that *Treasure Island* by Robert Louis Stevenson is the greatest pirate story ever written. Adventure, excitement, bravery. It's a story that captures the hearts and minds of youngsters and can continue to hold them into adulthood. According to the Internet Movie Database there were twelve screen or TV versions of this classic—the best was probably the aforementioned 1934 film with Wallace Beery as Long John.

a) explains that he is new and didn't get the memo. He asks if she can hold on another five minutes while he gathers some papers.

b) tells her the only meeting he will be attending is the one where she comes to HIS office, where he promises to be gentle with her. "Aye," Marvin adds, "ye be a saucy wench!"

Booty— A pirate's ill-gotten gains. The word has taken on a new connotation—a shapely posterior—but that still works in the context of Talk Like a Pirate Day. In fact, we briefly marketed women's underwear with the slogan PIRATE BOOTY across the back, but—sadly—they didn't sell terribly well, so we had to drop the women's underwear. No, wait, let's rephrase that.

Evaluation Point #2

If you answered (b) yet again, you seem to have been picking up pirattitude from somewhere. Are you related to Clark Gable or Viggo Mortensen? Unfortunately, our friends who answered (a) will need to see a doctor and have a "pire-x-ray" to see if there is any hope of some therapeutic intervention to stimulate their pirate gene.

Bowsprit— The forward-pointing spar at the bow of the ship. Or the forward-pointing part of an attractive woman or well-endowed man.

Let's take one last run at our story, shall we?

On the walk home, Marvin wondered what kind of car he would buy to go with his new position, increased income and feverishly hot, rich, new girlfriend. Suddenly, the neighbor's rabid mastiff, Adolf, charges the distracted man from behind. At a distance of about six feet, the dog releases a bloodcurdling "WOOF!" and is about to leap toward Marvin's unprotected neck. At this exact moment, Marvin:

a) loses control of his bladder and freezes motionless on the sidewalk as the huge, enraged dog sinks his sharklike teeth into the back of Marvin's neck, crushing his spinal cord and sending Marvin's body to the sidewalk where he breathes out his last and dies.

b) wheels around toward the leaping, gnarling nightmare of death and delivers a crushing head butt di-

rectly between the airborne canine's eyes. The dog lands in a heap on the sidewalk and rolls about yelping and trying to recover his footing. Marvin stands, fists clenched, arms akimbo, awaiting the second wave of an attack that never comes. Passersby later tell of a deep growl coming from the scene, which they attributed to the hound until discovering the sound persisted even after the beast had turned tail and run for the safety of an oncoming train.

Evaluation Point #3

Alright. If you selected (a) again, you not only have no hope of ever achieving pirattitude but clearly cannot distinguish a pattern of behavior and therefore cannot be trusted with any of your own life choices. Of course (b) is the choice. Who chooses dying on a sidewalk of a dog-inflicted spinal cord injury over classic victory complete with war-growling and standing arms akimbo? We're talking ARMS AKIMBO here, people!

Let's hope that this brief lesson and overview of pirattitude not only taught you valuable dog-fighting skills, but inspired you to take more pride in your work . . . and to do your paperwork in a timelier manner.

The Poster Boy for Pirattitude

Using his pocketknife, he amputated his arm below the elbow, put on a tourniquet and administered first aid. He then rigged anchors and fixed

Bosun, or bos'n— A shortened form of "boatswain," a ship's petty officer, midway in rank between the commissioned officers and the crew. There's nothing petty about a petty officer. Almost any old salt will tell you that it's really the bos'n who run the ship. Well, either the bos'n or the bos'n's mommy.

a rope to rappel to the floor of Blue John Canyon.

—*ROCKY MOUNTAIN NEWS*,
SATURDAY, MAY 3, 2003.

(Telephone rings at the Baurs' house.)

John *(Cheerfully)* Hello! Baur residence. John Baur speaking.

Mark Dude, you have to stop answering the phone like that. It's creepy.

John That's how I answer the phone. It's the way I was taught.

Mark It's creepy. You sound like a machine.

John *(Not nearly so cheerful)* Hi, Mark. What's up?

Mark I have the embodiment of pirattitude for you!

John Were we looking for it? I thought WE were the embodiment of pirattitude.

Mark Dude, just listen, there was this hiker—

John A biker? Like Lance Armstrong?

Mark No, just listen—there was this hiker guy and he got his arm stuck in a rockfall and after trying to free himself for a couple of days, he finally cut his own arm off with a pocketknife and some fairly determined bone breaking.

John Lance Armstrong would be the perfect embodiment of pirattitude—what has he won, like, seventeen straight Tour de Frances?

Mark No, dude, listen. This guy makes Lance Armstrong look like a pussy.

John You take that back!

Mark Never! Seriously, dude, would Lance Armstrong cut off his arm and rappel down a canyon and then spend the weekend partying with supermodels? I don't think so.

John Then you would be wrong. He would do all of that after giving himself superhuman doses of chemotherapy to fight off testicular cancer.

Mark Well, my hiker dude—a Mr. Aron Ralston—would.

John Spell it.

Mark A-R-O-N *(pause)* R-A-

John You don't spell "Aaron" A-R-O-N! That's just wrong.

Mark That's how we spell it from now on, because this guy has serious pirattitude.

John But not as much as Lance Armstrong.

Mark Would you forget Lance Armstrong—I'm not going to talk about Lance Armstrong until we can accurately refer to him as Lance Arm-GONE! *(long pause)* Because he cut it off with a pocketknife—

John I get it.

Mark You know—without an arm?

John Yeah, I get it.

Mark Dude, seriously, Ralston's story's got everything you'd want in a pirate story—sharp-edged weapons, mutilation, as well as "friggin' in the riggin'." I think we make Aron Ralston the poster boy for pirattitude!

John We don't have posters.

Brass monkey— A brass base with sixteen indentations for cannonballs, laid out in a square. This allowed a pyramid of thirty cannonballs to be stored near the guns without fear of their rolling about loose on the deck. Brass contracts faster and to a greater degree than iron, which the ammunition was made of, so when the temperature dropped too far too quickly, the brass indentations would shrink so much that the iron cannonballs would come right off the monkey. This is the source of the phrase, "It's cold enough to freeze the balls off a brass monkey." (Incidentally, we've been told this is a legend, that there's no truth in it. This would be an appropriate time to remind readers that we don't care. It's a good story.)

Mark What?

John I said, we don't have posters.

Mark What do we need posters for?

John You just said you wanted to make Aron Ralston the poster boy for pirattitude, but we don't have posters.

Mark It was a figure of—

John —of speech, I know, but if you're going to have a poster boy for pirattitude, shouldn't there be posters?

Mark Well, I suppose . . .

John I mean, a big damn poster with Lance Armstrong on it dressed up as a pirate—he could be balancing his bicycle on a French guy in one of those beret hats and—

Mark Like Mary Tyler Moore.

John What?

Mark Dude, like Mary Tyler Moore, when she flung her beret in the air?

John No. That was some sort of knit hat.

Mark Yeah, a knit beret.

John No. A knit hat—a beret, like a French guy would wear, would be made out of wool.

Mark What's "knit" made out of?

John What? Wait, what does this have to do with Lance Armstrong?

Mark Aron Ralston.

John Okay. But what does Mary Tyler Moore's hat have to do with either Lance Armstrong or Aron Ralston?

Mark I don't know. You're the one who brought it up.

John I was just saying that Lance Armstrong

Role Models for Today's Pirate Guy
Who Has Pirattitude, and Who Doesn't?

Has Pirattitude	**Sadly, Has No Pirattitude**
Avril Lavigne	Britney Spears
Brett Favre	Peyton Manning
Tonya Harding	Warren G. Harding
Katie Couric	Matt Lauer
The Rolling Stones	The BeeGees
Jimmy Buffett	Barry Manilow
Johnny Depp	Jonny Quest
Ruben Studdard	Clay Aiken
Donald Trump	Ken Lay
Hank Williams	Buck Owens
Tommy Chong	Cheech Marin
David Letterman	David Ogden Stiers
Rhett Butler	Ashley Wilkes
The Beastie Boys	The Backstreet Boys
Goofus	Gallant
Steve Martin	Carrot Top
Stephen Sondheim	Andrew Lloyd Webber
Chuck Yeager	Chuck Norris
Former Green Bay Packer Jerry Kramer	Former sitcom star Jerry Seinfeld
Tony Soprano	The late Tony Randall
Spider-Man	Batman
Macbeth	Hamlet
Bruce Springsteen	Bruce Hornsby
Bruce Campbell	Bruce Babbitt
Bruce Lee	Bruce Boxleitner
Robert the Bruce	Bruce Wayne

Broadside— When two ships fought, they maneuvered so that they could fire all the guns from one side of the ship at their opponent at the same time, thus vastly increasing the chance that one might actually hit the other. Counterbalance was also important. This led to the less popular phrases "Fatties to starboard!" and "Fatties to port!"

would be a great poster boy for pirattitude.

Mark We don't have posters!

John That's what I said. WAIT! We're sounding like *The Bickersons*. Do you want to sound like *The Bickersons*?

Mark *(long pause)* No.

John Can we just agree that both Lance Armstrong and your hiker guy—

Mark Aron Ralston

John Right, Aron Ralston, would both make splendid poster boys for pirattitude?

Mark If we had posters.

John If we had posters.

(Silence)

Mark So would Mary Tyler Moore.

John I'm taking Max to school now.

Mark Seriously, Mary Tyler Moore would be a terrific poster girl for pirattitude.

John I'm hanging up.

Mark Just think about it.

(Click)

Mark John? John? *(pause)* I'll take that as an "I'll think about it."

Things with Pirattitude

The inanimate things you surround yourself with can speak volumes about your level of pirattitude. Here are a few items that you might want to check.

Has Pirattitude	**Sadly, Has No Pirattitude**
Beer	Drinks with umbrellas
George Foreman Grill	Cuisinart
Duct tape	Hot glue gun
Mardi Gras	Macy's Thanksgiving Day Parade
Pizza	Veggie pizza with wheat crust, goat cheese and artichokes
Coffee	Orange Frappuccino with soy
Cirrhosis of the liver	Lactose intolerance
Bloodred	Dusty rose
Aunt Jemima*	Mrs. Butterworth
The Rocky Horror Picture Show	*Cats*
Godfather I & II	*Godfather III*

*The Aunt Jemima Web site, www.auntjemima.com, provides product information, healthy eating tips and pancake fun facts.

3

Get Yer Pirate Name Here!

In Which the buccaneer wannabe gets his or her very own pirate name!

So ye be a pirate, eh? How do ye want to be listed on the ship's crew manifest?

Since launching the holiday and our Web site, we've received many requests from people asking us to bestow a pirate name on them. This surprised us a bit, since pirate names are kind of personal, and we always felt that, with enough pirattitude, any buccaneer worth his or her salt ought to claim his or her own name, rather than meekly

The Pirate Guys' Name Generator

Column A, third letter of your first name; Column B, second letter of your last name; Column C, last letter of your last name.* (Our apologies beforehand to anyone named Dave Smith.)

Column A	Column B	Column C
a - Dread	a - Patch	a - Stormwatcher
b - Salty	b - Pistol	b - Fireship
c - Vicious	c - Dogwatch	c - Culverin
d - Mad	d - Scourge	d - Sassmouth
e - Soggy	e - Squid	e - Ridingcrop
f - Crusty	f - Big Boat	f - Morgan
g - Greasy	g - Scuppers	g - Flint
h - Dangerous	h - Cheesebeard	h - Salamislacks
i - Sinister	i - Boots	i - Le Bastardi
j - Blind	j - Bread	j - the Interior Decorator
k - Scurvy	k - Bowsprit	k - Littlejib
l - Bloody	l - Spyglass	l - Abattoir
m- Dastardly	m - Arse	m - Oubliette
n - Curly	n - Cutlass	n - the Well-Endowed
o - Furious	o - Chains	o - Chamberpot
p - Flinty	p - Dirk	p - Mizzenmast
q - Saucy	q - Slash	q - the Proctologist
r - Squinty	r - Rumpot	r - Broadside
s - Slippery	s - Hookhand	s - Slappy
t - Fancy	t - Headwound	t - Tankard
u - Crusty	u - Blunderbuss	u - Tungsten
v - Smelly	v - Barnacle	v - Cavalier
w -Red	w - Skipper	w - Johnson
x - Black	x - Hammock	x - Shipburner
y - One-eared	y - Gunner	y - Slowmatch
z - Sharp	z - Dog	z - Gunnels

*In the rare instance that someone has only two letters in his or her last name (like "Ng" and, well, we can only think of "Ng") we invoke the "Ng Exception," which states that anyone whose last name contains only two letters takes the last name of "Ng."

Bilge rat— A denizen of the lowest, dirtiest, slimiest level of a ship. A lot of guy humor involves insulting your buddies to prove your friendship. It's important that everyone understand you are smarter, more powerful and much luckier with the wenches than they are. Since "bilge rat" is a pretty dirty thing to call someone, by all means use it on your friends.

Bucko— Friend, mate, buddy. Homey, if you will. Like so many pirate pleasantries and endearments, works well with a possessive "me" in front, such as, "Well done, me bucko," when your friend buys a round of drinks. If you buy us a round of drinks, we'll call you "me bucko," too.

asking a stranger to assign one. At the very least, a good pirate nickname ought to come from your mates, people who know you and can taunt you with a name reflecting what they perceive as your weaknesses or more "colorful" characteristics.

It's up to you (or your shipmates) whether your name is fierce, funny or whimsical. Obviously the names we chose—Cap'n Slappy and Ol' Chumbucket—leave something to be desired in the fierceness department. As the founders of a holiday, we wanted to be clear that we recognized just how peculiar the idea of a day devoted to talking like a pirate was, so we chose whimsical names. It's worked for us, but there are times, mostly in bars, when we kind of wish we'd chosen something more along the lines of Bloody Hook Summers or Evil Eye John. Well, what's done is done and there are no do-overs.

But as we say, we got a LOT of requests for names. We wanted to be sure that anyone who wants a name gets one, so after assigning them somewhat randomly, we came up with a system. There are several ways to use the matrix on page 23. If you are feeling totally uninspired or in need of our firm hand in your naming, then follow the directions. Or, just follow the directions for Column A and Column C, and insert your own name in the middle.

But if you just need some ideas, use the list for inspiration, taking whatever words speak to you. Hell, throw a dart at the thing for all we care. Remember—you're a pirate! You don't need OUR permission to take a dangerous-sounding name!

Who's in Charge Here?

We get a lot of mail, and many of those correspondents sign with their pirate name. And one thing we've noticed is that almost all call themselves "Captain" something or other. It's almost universally Captain "This," "That" or "the Other Thing."

We can't *all* be captains, can we? Certainly there has to be a crew.

Now, it's a fact that pirate crews were democratic—electing their captain and quartermaster from among their number. A pirate captain had to be fiercely intimidating or political or just lucky to stay in the position for long. And that's how we'd advise settling things. When you get together with your crew on September 19 to celebrate Talk Like a Pirate Day, hold a vote to see who gets to be called "Captain" for the next year. It could be fun, and will give the unsuccessful candidates something to brood over for twelve months.

Henry Morgan
Nickname: King of the Pirates
Rum: Delicious
Worked: Both sides of the street
Job security: Excellent
Buckle: Swashed
In the late seventeenth century, Morgan was the top of the heap, the never-crowned king of the pirates. Not only was he acknowledged as the leader of all the pirates sailing out of Jamaica, he was also for a time simultaneously the English vice admiral charged with cleaning out the pirates. In this dual role Henry Morgan became the terror of all Spaniards in the West Indies. In one such raid he sacked two cities, took more than 50,000 English pounds in booty, and routed three Spanish men-o'-war. On another he captured prizes worth more than 100,000 pounds. Unfortunately, at that point England and Spain were no longer at war, and Morgan was recalled to England and thrown into prison. But Charles II was so impressed with his tales that he knighted him and sent him back to Jamaica to rid the Caribbean of pirates.

4

What Is YOUR Pi-Q?

In Which the Pirate Guys rate your piratical intelligence, and make fun of you just because.

Okay, so now we know you've got pirattitude, or at least the makings of it. Now we need to get a bead on how smart you are, pirate-wise.

There's only ONE NAME in intelligence testing—it's Stanford-Binet! Alright, so that's two names. In point of fact it is a name of a place (Stanford University) and a French fella, Alfred Binet, who wanted to know just how smart French people were in 1905. In 1916, Stanford professor Lewis Terman wanted to have Binet dumb down his test to see how smart Americans were. In true American fashion, he was so confident in the new tool that he decided not to put his own name on it, but rather the name of his employer. Americans have been getting dumber ever since.

"But wait just a doll-garned minute there, mister!" you may be saying—go ahead, say it; it will feel good—"Isn't that test culturally biased and thereby rendered impotent?" To which we answer, "How did you get from 'doll-garned' to 'thereby rendered impotent' in one sentence?" Look, we all know that intelligence testing is culturally, ethnically and multigenerationally biased. But that has not stopped us from pigeonholing millions of children and assigning them to a life of backbreaking drudgery at low wages simply because a fancy French test tells us that they don't have the brains God gave a peanut. Without those "under one hundreds," who would we "over one hundreds" have to make our Sausage McMuffins with Egg? Hmmm?

With this in mind, we have developed our own tool, the Pi-Q Test, which will measure your piratical intelligence and help us know whether to place you above deck in a decision-making position or below deck in the chamber pot–emptying section. It is our sincere hope that we have addressed the inequities in past intelligence-gathering tools. Some have called our test "sexist yet sexy" as well as "pirate-centric." We respond to our critics with a

William Kidd
Favorite weapon: Bucket
Luck: All bad
Little-known fact: Wore his hair in a pompadour so large that it sometimes caught the wind like a sail, adding five knots to his ship's speed

A hard luck story if ever we've heard one. Kidd, a New Yorker, left England with letters of marque permitting him to prey on the shipping of France and Spain but specifying he was to leave alone the shipping of England and her allies. The expedition was all unofficial, his authority a secret. Well, the crew got restless. After putting down one mutiny by killing the leader with a bucket, Kidd eventually gave in to the crew and captured ships he wasn't entitled to. Kidd was eventually abandoned by his crew and made his way back to England to defend his reputation. Bad move. After a one-sided trial Kidd was convicted of murder (for killing the leading mutineer) and was hanged in 1701.

hearty "Aye, that we be!" and a savage pummelin' with our fists and foreheads.

So if you have your quills ready, please respond as best you can to the following questions. You have only twenty-five minutes. Do not take too much time on any one question and do not guess. You may use a calculator; fat lot of good it will do you. At least one item in every question has a negative value number. If you do not understand these instructions, please turn your test back in and you will receive a sharp blow to the back of the skull.

Begin.

Beauty— The best possible pirate address for a woman. Always preceded by "me," as in, "C'mere, me beauty," or "me proud beauty," or even "me buxom beauty," to one particularly well-endowed. This should never be confused with "me pretty," which is a phrase that was copyrighted by the Wicked Witch of the West. Rest assured, if you use it without her permission, she'll get you—and your little dog, too!

1. Hook is to hand as:
   a) Jack is to Jill
   b) peg is to leg
   c) Jack is to Eddie
   d) Jill is with the entire fleet
2. Which of the following does not belong?
   a) Starboard
   b) Reggie
   c) Rush Limbaugh
   d) Lefty Louis Lazario
3. Which phrase best fits the description of being the opposite of "Avast thar, ye scurvy dogs!"
   a) "Keep going, gentlemen, don't stop for little ol' me!"
   b) "Wait, I have good news for you about our Heavenly Father!"
   c) "Stop that! I am not a cuddler!"
   d) "Run for your lives! We're being attacked by children with daisies!"

Laddie— Ostensibly a term of affection, with a touch of paternalism ("Aye, you're a good laddie"). Because it's a diminutive, it's actually a bit of a slam. It's a backhanded way to point out that you're more mature, wise, manly and successful with women than your friend could ever hope to be. So use it often.

4. If a sloop with a northeast wind of six knots sailing from San Juan to Saint Kitts carrying twenty-three pirates weighing on average eight and a half stone along with ten six-pound cannons and enough food and rum for eighteen days intersects the English frigate HMS *Unmerciful Coldsore* with forty guns, a crew of 132 plus 100 well-trained marines with Sharps rifles and enough ammunition to launch a successful invasion of Norway, given that there is only one yardarm in Saint Kitts, how long will it take to hang all twenty-three pirates?
   a) Three hours
   b) Five hours
   c) They will all have been killed in the sea battle.
   d) The pirate sloop miraculously outran the frigate, sought refuge on a deserted island and founded the country of Pirattica, which didn't last long as they had failed to bring along any women.
5. If x is a real integer and y represents a complete set of items, then which of the following is not true?
   a) $x+X(y)+y=n$
   b) $Y= x-y(X) + 17$
   c) $Xy+ -y(x) = Yx-+x(y)$
   d) If there is an X then there MUST be buried treasure.
6. What is the fallacy in this story? Young William the powder monkey has just slashed his way through fourteen French pirates during a boarding. Exhausted, he finally reaches

Cannon— The ordnance on ships of the day tended to be somewhat diverse. In the fifteenth and sixteenth centuries it was a rare artillery piece that could be counted on to throw two balls the same distance in the same general direction. The likelihood that two cannon on the same ship would be fairly evenly matched was almost nil. Add to that the slight variances between the size and shape of each ball and you begin to see why a pirate's best chance was to get as close alongside a ship as possible and trade broadsides. Once the prey was disabled, they could board and capture her. There were many, many kinds of cannon—culverins, demiculverins, monkeys, ship-smashers, mankillers. It's too confusing to try to track 'em. Call 'em all cannon.

the French captain, who surrenders his sword and his ship to the young English pirate. William spares the French captain his life and the two become good friends.

a) The English and the French can NEVER be friends.
b) A powder monkey would never have a sword and therefore couldn't "slash" anyone.
c) Powder monkeys are mythical beasts, like sea serpents, unicorns and Irish setters.
d) It was all made up for this silly test.

7. Which phrase best fits the description of meaning the opposite of "I'll be splicin' the mainbrace when the sun is o'er the yardarm!"
   a) "Say, a cup of tea would jolly well hit the spot at two this afternoon."
   b) "This is a 'dry' pirate ship—temperance now, temperance ever!"
   c) "Doc! I woke up this morning and a belayin' pin was in me booty!"
   d) "These new trousers ride uncomfortably high in the crotch!"
8. Which of the following seems to be the most unlikely coupling?
   a) Blackbeard and Grand Champion black standard poodle Mr. Wigglesworth the Fourth
   b) Stede Bonnet and the Vienna Boys' Choir
   c) Anne Bonney and a pack of roughhousing kindergarteners from St. Ignacio's School for Cross-Dressers

   d) Calico Jack Rackham and a can of dolphin-safe tuna
9. Hempen jig is to dance as:
   a) kissing the gunner's daughter is to making out
   b) billet is to ballet
   c) Irish is to sobriety
   d) frisky is to kitten
10. Which of the following does not belong?
   a) An eye patch
   b) A parrot
   c) A brace of pistols
   d) Leg warmers

Alright, me hearties, put down yer quills. Since we cannot be bothered to score each of these individually, we have supplied ye with yer own scoring guide. It is located on page 74. Remember, we are on the honor system, so be sure to score your Pi-Q accurately. (We wouldn't want your first act as a pirate to be dishonest, now would we?)

5

Pirate Talk: How to Make It Work for You

In Which we present the basics of pirate lingo, and show you how to back it up with action.

What good is it being full of pirattitude if nobody knows it? None! No one will believe you're a pirate if you walk into your office or country club and say something like, "Golly, Chester! Some rude person has parked his Beamer in my private space!" No, you'll need a lot more growling, swaggering and cursing if you want to be taken seriously on Talk Like a Pirate Day, or any other day, for that matter.

Tell people that September 19 is Talk Like a Pirate Day and chances are most of them will reply, "Arrr!" Some will say "Huh?" or "Are you feeling okay?" or even, "No, seriously, are you feeling okay?" But most—probably 97 percent—will say "Arrr!"

And for a lot of them, that's as far as it goes. Just "Arrr!", because that's all the pirate talk they know.

We've gotta work on that, because "Arrr," as fine an utterance as it may be, just isn't enough. As an interjection it works. Growling out a prolonged "Arrr" may give you just the time you need to think of how to articulate your message in piratical terms, sort of like a politician stalls for time by saying "my fellow Americans." But a vocabulary limited to "Arrr" isn't enough. Now that we've figured out why to talk like a pirate (it's fun, remember?) we need to focus on the how. Step one: Go on beyond "Arrr!"

But let's start with the origin of "Arrr!" In fact, where did pirate talk come from? There have been pirates as long as there has been shipping. Julius Caesar got kidnapped by pirates, for the love of Morgan! There have been pirates from every country with a coastline, and probably most of the rest as well. There are pirates today, and they're not much to laugh at. History's pirates have spoken every language.

Henry Every
Nickname: Long Ben Avery, and not because he had big feet
Career: Colorful
Strong suit: Irony
Died: Penniless

Long Ben Avery signed aboard a ship outfitted to stop pirates in the Caribbean, then mutinied and led his followers instead to the Indian Ocean where, joined by several other ships, they took the greatest single prize of any pirate ever, the treasure ship of the Grand Moghul. Millions of pounds in gold and jewels were gained in a single attack. Avery then gave his partners the slip and escaped with the fantastic treasure. But because so much of the booty was in jewels, Avery couldn't just show up and sell them without being accused of being a pirate. He had to work through merchants, who proved to be just as piratical as he was. He gave them the diamonds to sell. They accepted the jewels but never paid him, threatening to turn him in if he made a fuss. He died without even the price of a coffin to his name.

Careen— Careening was one of those things you had to do periodically to keep a ship floating, but to do it you had to get the ship out of water, and that made it pretty dangerous to pirates. The ship would be run aground in a shallow bay. Then the pirates would wait for the tide to go down, exposing as much of the hull as possible. The ship would be pulled to one side, using block and tackle and brute strength, and the exposed surface would be scraped clean of barnacles and other debris that hurt speed and maneuverability. The planks would then be pitched or tarred or painted. The ship would be pulled over to the other side and the process repeated. As you can imagine, it was long and difficult work, and the time spent with the ship on the beach was time the pirates were exposed without much chance to defend themselves.

But when we say "talk like a pirate," you immediately think of the swashbuckling buccaneers of the seventeenth and eighteenth centuries, marauding against the Spanish Plate Fleet and the English navy throughout the Caribbean and on the other side of the world. And you can hear them growling things like "Arrr, me hearties!" and "Well, blow me down for an old sea calf!" in an accent usually mistaken for cockney. Ever wonder why?

Meet Robert Newton

It's all because of Robert Newton. He's the reason we think of pirates talking the way we do. He did it single-handedly.

English character actor Robert Newton was a ham and, as one critic enthused, "a succulent one!" We say that with a great deal of respect and admiration. Subtlety had no place in his actor's bag of tricks. "Over the top" is the only way to describe his style. He came by his accent honestly enough. Newton was from Cornwall, England's southernmost tip of land.

So when he played Long John Silver in the 1951 Disney version of *Treasure Island,* he drew on his Cornish background and its distinctive dialect to make the peg-legged pirate something truly memorable. He came up with a performance that was all growls and rolling eyes and "Arrr, me hearties." It made an indelible impression. Even people who never saw Newton's inimitable performance know that THAT'S what a pirate is supposed to sound like.

To pay the man his due for his influence on piratical speech, we have declared him the patron saint of Talk Like a Pirate Day. Make sure you purchase your St. Robert medals at our gift shop in the lobby. In the unlikely event of a water landing, they can be used as a flotation device.

We'll close this section with our favorite Robert Newton line. You'll be able to hear the proper growl in every syllable.

"Them what dies will be the lucky ones! Arrrr!"

The Five A's

"Arrr!" is one of what we call "the Five A's." We call them this because that's the letter they begin with, and our crack mathematics team assures us that there are five of them.

These exclamations are the glue that binds together pirate lingo. Even if you don't know a bunghole from a broadside or a mizzenmast from a maidenhead, you can still give your conversation a little pirate panache by injecting these exclamations into your landlubber lexicon.

Avast—"Stop and give attention." It can be used in a sense of surprise: "Whoa! Get a load of that!" when a beautiful woman walks into the room. "Avast! Check out the bowsprit on that fine beauty!" you might say.

Ahoy—"Hello!" Any inference beyond "Hello!"

is simply vocal inflection and has nothing to do with the real meaning of the word.

Aye—"Why, yes, I agree most heartily with everything you just said or did."

Aye, aye—"I'll get right on that, sir, as soon as my break is over." We've never heard any similarly colorful expressions for "no," perhaps because pirates were the type you didn't want to say no to.

Arrr—This one is often confused with "arrgh," which is of course the sound you make when you sit on a belaying pin. "Arrr!" can mean, variously, "Yes," "I agree," "I'm happy," "I'm enjoying this beer," "My team is winning," "My team is losing," "I saw that television show, it sucked," "I am here and alive" and "That was a clever remark you or I just made." And those are just a few of the myriad possibilities of "Arrr!" It's a little bit like the pirate version of "Oy," that indispensable Yiddish word that has almost as many meanings as there are ways to pronounce it.

To give the proper "Arrr," start by standing with your feet apart, about shoulder width, and arms akimbo. (This means with your fists—not palms, fists!—planted on your hips, elbows wide. If we ever decide to become professional wrestlers, we think Arms Akimbo would be a GREAT wrasslin' name.) Then start a rumble in your belly and, with all the pirattitude you can muster, let it rise up your throat and burst out gutturally—"Aaaarrrr!" You've got it!

Curses! Foiled Again!

Sometimes ye've just gotta curse. There are times when saying "shucks" or "darn" won't cut it, won't give you that release you need. As Mark Twain (another close personal friend of ours) once said, "Under certain circumstances, profanity provides a relief denied even to prayer."

In extreme conditions—when your team has blown a seventeen-point lead in the fourth quarter, or your friend has left tire ruts in your front lawn, or your dog has jumped up on the table and stolen the pot roast—cut loose. Here's how.

Pick one or two items from the modifier list on the left (or more, if blowing that seventeen-point lead caused your team to miss the playoffs). Then pick a noun from the list on the right (one should be sufficient, but don't let us cramp your style), take a deep breath, screw up your face and shout it out.

Modifiers	**Nouns**
Lily-livered	Landlubber
Barnacle-bottomed	Rum pot
Chum-swillin'	Bilge monkey
Kelp-festooned	Kraaken
Rusty-hooked	Son of a sea cow
Fish-sniffing	Gull-dropping collector
Weevil-eatin'	Fancy lad
Figurehead-fondlin'	Sheep shagger
Albatross-huggin'	Sea dog
Hornswogglin'	Monkey dancer

continued...

Hempen halter— The hangman's noose. When celebrating Talk Like a Pirate Day at work, you could use the phrase to refer to the tie you have knotted around your neck. And when the boss finds out that your accounting errors have cost the company billions, you can put your hempen halter to good use—strangling your boss.

Modifiers	Nouns
Frog-lickin'	Cannon fodder
Bilge-belchin'	Fishmonger
Wench-wrestlin'	Treasure dropper
Poop-swabbin'	Parrot spanker
Grog-guzzlin'	Thicky
Porthole-pluggin'	Dirty ol' salt
Seaweed-smokin'	Second assistant cabin boy

There, doesn't that feel better?

In a pinch, a pirate cursin' competition can be a fun event at your Pirate Gala or Wednesday evening prayer meeting.

Pirate Vocabulary

In the office

Two warnings: First, your boss is probably one of those people who have all kinds of expectations about "proper office behavior" and not "scaring" the clients. She or he probably operates under that quaint notion that while you're at work you'll actually work. Ha! For what they pay you?

Second: Pirate talk does have a certain sauciness, as you will have noticed by now, and in the wrong environment—almost anything outside a locker room, really—one person's wacky, fun-loving zaniness is another's sexual harassment, which, as we all know, is actionable. So let's keep things in control. Neither Mark nor John particularly wants to be hauled into court as an accessory.

When we get hauled into court, we want to be the centerpiece, not the garnish.

Armed with your new sense of pirattitude, you can apply pirate phrases to all kinds of things. Here's how that might work in the office.

The bilge—Where the lower level employees work, the cubicle farm. Your desk is probably there.

Chart a course—Develop a mission statement or strategy, or generally take part in any useless activity.

Maroon—If you've been handed an assignment or project that's not properly funded and which will strand you with no support or chance of success, you've been marooned.

Captain's quarters—Obviously, the CEO's office.

The goat locker—This is the quarters of the bos'n, quartermaster or whatever petty officer actually runs the ship. In your case, it'd be the office of your immediate supervisor.

Hempen halter—The tie you have to wear to work every day.

Grog—A mixture of rum and water given to sailors every day. In the office, this might be that mixture of coffee grounds and lukewarm water that passes for coffee in the break room. If you're clever, you might mix some rum into it as well.

Tot—A cup, sometimes worn on a chain around the neck, into which sailors received their ration of grog every day. This is how you might refer to your coffee cup during your morning break.

Suck the monkey— Sailors sometimes augmented their official rum ration by buying coconuts from locals at ports where they stopped. The coconuts had had the milk removed and replaced with rum. The nuts themselves were said to resemble a monkey's head, so sailors drinking from a coconut were said to "suck the monkey."

Scuttlebutt—At the back of the ship—on the poop—there sat a barrel, or "butt," that held water or grog. Sailors gathered there during a lull in the action and gossiped—not unlike the modern watercooler. "What's the poop?" "Anybody heard any good scuttlebutt?" These questions echo across the years—up through the vent and into your boss's office.

In church

Every few years, Talk Like a Pirate Day will fall on a Sunday. We've always believed there's no harm in a little levity among the faithful, but even we have been somewhat surprised by the way ministers and members have pitched in to make the Lord's day and our day work together. Churches all over the country and around the world have held special services with pirate themes. Here's a handy list of a few church terms and their nautical translations.

Church	**Aboard ship**
Amen	Aye, aye!
Pulpit	The poop deck
Full immersion baptism	Keelhauling
The choir loft	The crow's nest
Bounty	Booty
Pastor	Cap'n
Deacon	Bos'n
Communion host	Hardtack
Communion wine	Grog

The Rev. Cap'n Slappy's Suggested Pirate Sermons

Did you know that Cap'n Slappy, on top of everything else, is an ordained minister? Well, he is, of the online variety, but legally empowered to conduct weddings and everything! (Contact him through our Web site—www.talklikeapirate.com—for his incredibly exorbitant fee for conducting your wedding!) Here are a few of his suggested sermons for those special years when Talk Like a Pirate Day falls on a Sabbath.

Loaves and Fishes: Rationing Is for the Unfaithful
Blessed Are the Meek—For They Shall Be Pummeled and Plundered
Ten Things I Would Do If I Knew I Would Rise from the Dead in Three Days!
Walking on Water—and Other Things to Do When You're Drunk
David and Goliath—How a Swift Sloop Can Take a Man-O'-War, and Other Applicable Lessons
When God Said "Don't Fornicate" He Wasn't Talkin' about Us
Thar Be Too Much Goddam Blasphemin' Goin' On!
Hell and Other Places That Seem Nice When Compared to Service in the British Navy
The Apostle Paul: The Blackbeard of the Early Church
Tithing—Give the Big Cap'n in the Sky His Share

Chumbucket— Chum is fish bait, usually ground-up, oily fish, often with blood and guts. It's spread over the water to attract feeding fish, which are then caught and turned into more chum. This is what mariners from time immemorial called "the Circle of Chum." The fish seem to like it. And the chumbucket, obviously, is the bucket the chum is kept in. Referring to something—say, a restaurant or bowl of chowder or your sister-in-law's meticulously clean bathroom—as a chumbucket is clearly not a compliment, although guys will find the concept irresistible.

At the Doctor's Office

Nurse	Me angel of mercy
Take off your shirt	Hoist yer mains'l
Proctological exam	Visit the poop deck
Turn your head and cough	Surrender or die!
Viagra	Sail-raisin' crew
Hypodermic needle	Harpoon
Anesthesia	Sharp rap with a belayin' pin
X-ray	Treasure map

6

Pirates on the Prowl

In Which the aspiring pirate learns how to use the lingo for a vital task: picking up dates.

John was talking to his son Max about an incident that occurred that day in kindergarten. Max had fallen during recess while he was chasing girls.

"Why were you chasing girls?" John asked.

Brethren of the Coast— A name pirates in the Caribbean gave themselves. They formed a loose association, and never (or at least rarely) attacked or stole from each other. This seems as good a place as any to mention that the buccaneer communities of the Caribbean were often homosexual. So if a group of gay friends wanted to celebrate Talk Like a Pirate Day, they could bill themselves as "the Brethren of the Coast."

Max, with a tone of exasperation, explained, "Because I'm on the Boys Chasing Girls team." Then, with a furrowed brow, he mused, "They're hard to catch."

Amen, Max! Yes, girls ARE hard to catch, and it doesn't get any easier when you grow up, if you ever do. We know guys well into their sixties who are STILL on the Boys Chasing Girls team, and not having significantly better luck (as measured by the number of times actually hooking up versus incidents of going home alone) than Max. Sure, there are a few guys who seem to have unqualified success in this department, who never seem to have trouble meeting and getting together with partners, and we advocate beating them all with sticks, because it just isn't fair.

Whether you're on the Guys Chasing Girls team, the Women Chasing Guys team, or on the team of either men or women chasing one of the same, it never seems to get any easier.

Well, we're here to help. It's a well-known fact that pirates are far more virile, handsome and—most importantly—successful in attracting dates than other people. And we're here to pass the secrets of our legendary success on to you.

(And don't listen to those people who know us. They'll quibble, suggesting that "legendary" applies to us only in an ironic way, and that "success with women" really ought to mean scoring occasionally. Well, don't believe a word of it. They're just jealous. We're legendary! Legendary, we say!!!!)

First let's look at a typical night at a typical bar, tavern or other watering spot, and see how things might go for a member of the Boys Chasing Girls team.

He walks in and sizes the place up. After one or two drinks to bolster his courage, he picks his prey, the most beautiful woman in the bar. He sidles over and strikes up a conversation.

Him: Hey, babe, what's your sign?
Her: Stop.
Him: Ha ha! No, seriously, do you think if I wore glasses I could see you home?
Her: You'll be lucky to see tomorrow.
Him: *(still not getting it)* I love a woman with a sense of humor. So, is this seat taken?
Her: No, but if you sit in it, this one will become vacant.
Him: C'mon. I know how to please a woman.
Her: Then please leave me alone.

And so it goes, with him trying with increasing desperation to score and her continuing to shoot him down in flames. Is that the way it always goes? It's hard to say. Our own experience is that the smoother the pickup line, the less likely the potential picker-upper is to succeed. It is the more confident hunter, the one who doesn't feel he or she needs glib patter, who is the quicker picker-upper.

With that in mind, let's look at some tips for how the Pirate Guy (or Gal) might improve the odds for success on September 19.

Eustace the Monk
Career: 1205–1217
Talents: Accessorizing otherwise bland robes
Eustace the Monk was not a classic pirate in the tradition of Henry Morgan or Black Bart Roberts. He preceded them by almost four centuries, entering the field when controlling the seas mostly meant controlling the Straits of Dover. He worked for King John of England, then traded sides for a price and sailed for the French. These were the days when being captain of a pirate ship often meant commanding no more than a flat-bottomed barge for transporting troops. That being the case, you might wonder why we've included him here. Simple. We LOVE the name Eustace the Monk. Really, Anybody "the Monk" works for us. Try it. Robert the Monk. Adelbert the Monk. Slappy the Monk (not because he likes being celibate—it just usually works out that way). Monk the Monk.

Prepare for Action

Cat-o'-nine-tails— A particularly vicious whip used for flogging. The cat was also sometimes known as "the gunner's daughter" or "the captain's daughter." In the old sea chanty, "What Do You Do with a Drunken Sailor," there is the line, "Give him a taste of the captain's daughter." Turns out what the song is calling for is a lot less pleasant than you thought, huh?

Splice the mainbrace— We are given on good authority that this means "have a drink," as in "Let's drop anchor in that alehouse and splice the mainbrace." We have to confess we have no idea why it might mean this, or what splicing the mainbrace might really mean. It sounds like some repair work you might have to do to some really important thing, and if you're really in need of a drink, that could be a reasonable metaphor. Yeah, that could be it.

No self-respecting pirate will go into combat without the proper gear and a vessel that's shipshape. When a heavily armed pirate ship with the Jolly Roger flapping in the breeze bore down on a merchantman, often the sight was so terrifying that the prey gave up without firing a shot. So why do so many guys go into singles' bars unprepared?

Now, let's be clear that the analogy is very incomplete. To begin with, the goals of a pirate ship and a guy in a singles' bar are different—the pirates want to loot and plunder by force. In the singles' scene, that's not just a no-no; that's illegal. (And we don't want to hear the whole "raping and pillaging" cliché. Raping IS NOT OKAY! Do not joke about raping. If you joke about raping, expect a savage beating from Cap'n Slappy's fists and forehead. Do we all understand this? Good.) Someone in a bar or other singles' scene is trying to *smooth-talk* his intended into accompanying him in what should be a good time for all.

Here's Cap'n Slappy's four-point checklist for how to prepare, and how to carry yourself for the maximum chance at success and the minimum risk of embarrassment when you are wooing.

Rule 1—First let's rule out obvious hygiene deficits. Take that bath! Wear a clean shirt, if you have one. Invest in deodorant. And would it kill ye to brush yer teeth now and again, and maybe even floss?

Rule 2—Never appear to be "needy." Wenches

will have no respect for a pirate who begs for it. Present an aloof (but fresh-smelling) air. Give her the impression that you could do without her or her kind. As a show of your aloofness, kiss a fancy lad full on the mouth and let her see you do it. Nothing screams "come hither" to a wench like the notion that ye may fancy the lads a bit too much. We don't know why this is, but it is.

Rule 3—Get in touch with the comic inside you. Wenches love to laugh. Try walking into the mizzenmast while looking another direction, or slipping in spilled chum. Humor is the best knickers-removal system known to man. With the right joke or anecdote, you will have her bloomers under your bunk in no time.

Rule 4—Above all, act like you've been there before. Experience is not nearly so important as the appearance of experience.

But first things first. Get that bath! And maybe a couple of Botox injections.

Cap'n Slappy's Rule for Wenches Seeking Company—Just name the place, time and degree of undressedness ye want and most of the time ye'll find a taker in mere minutes. If this doesn't work, lower your standards.

Scouring (and Scoring on) the Seas

When a pirate ship was searching for booty to plunder, the captain would steer a course for the

Spanish Main, crisscrossing the trade routes for likely ships. In other words—and attend closely—they went where the booty was likely to be!

The same is absolutely true when searching for booty today. Go where booty is likely to be found! Great Nelson's ghost! You'd think this would be obvious. But how many times have we heard guys complaining that they can't find dates, only to learn that these guys work in an office full of men and married women, and on the rare occasions when they go out, they're out with their buddies at a sports bar? Or women who are looking for guys and spend their days working in, say, a dress shop, where the only men to enter are likely under the strict control of their wives or girlfriends? Why else would men BE there, for crying out loud? Alright, so there are SOME men who might be there of their own accord, but most women would be disinclined to seek them out for a date.

Go where the booty is! If you're a single woman looking for men, don't go to the mall. Try a sports bar or get a friend to help you organize a poker party with a few of her male acquaintances. It'll look all innocent and fun, just a night of cards. But it's your chance to launch a surprise attack. And by surprise attack we mean getting all drunk and kissy.

When your co-author John was in high school, he took some ribbing from friends when he signed up for the cooking class. But it was obvious—that's where the girls were! Sure enough, he was one of three guys in a class with twenty-seven girls. It worked pretty well.

Bunghole— Stop snickering. Victuals on a ship, particularly the water and rum, were stored in wooden casks. The stopper in the barrel is called the bung, and the hole into which it fits is the bunghole. That's all. It sounds a lot worse than it is, doesn't it? When sitting down for a meal on Talk Like a Pirate Day you might loudly growl, "Well, let's see what crawled out of the bunghole!" This remark will be followed by the sound of your companions putting down their cutlery and backing away from the table. Good! More for you!

Anyone sailing in the waters of a singles' bar pretty much knows what he or she is getting into. So you can hope to at least have a chance for the thrill of the chase, as long as you remember that many people there may be ready to repel boarders.

Pickup Lines

We came up with the list of pirate pickup lines as a lark. Well, no, to tell the absolute truth it was part of a determined effort to attract the attention of a late-night television show. Hasn't worked yet, but we haven't completely given up hope. Anyway, the list got a lot of laughs on our Web site, but also some complaints. Where were the pickup lines for women? Where were the lines to be used on persons of the same sex?

Well, we're just a couple of guys, and that's what our experience is limited to. And we think most of the original list would work for any possible permutation or coupling you can imagine, but what do we know? So, in an effort to be inclusive, we've devised additional lists we hope help. Whichever line you try, make sure you "own" it. The words may be ours, but the passion and naughty inflection have to come from you.

Good luck and happy hunting!

Top Ten Pickup Lines for Male Pirates

10. Avast, me proud beauty! Wanna know why my Roger is so Jolly?

Monkey pump— A bit of straw used to sneak drinks from the grog barrels. Legend has it that after Horatio Nelson was killed at the Battle of Trafalgar and his body stored in a rum barrel for the return to England, some sailors, knowing there was rum in the barrel but not knowing about Nelson, used monkey pumps to sneak drinks. That's how rum came to be known as "Nelson's Blood" among British seamen.

9. That's the finest pirate booty I've ever laid eyes on.
8. Come on up to me cabin and see me urchins.
7. Yes, that is a hornpipe in my pocket and I am happy to see you.
6. I'd love to drop anchor in your lagoon.
5. Pardon me, but would ye mind if I fired me cannon through yer porthole?
4. How'd you like to scrape the barnacles off of me rudder?
3. Ye know, darlin', I'm 97 percent chum free.
2. Well, blow me down!
1. Prepare to be boarded.

The lasses rarely have a need for pickup lines, but there has been a great deal of demand for such, and we always do our best to meet the demands of the wenches.

Top Ten Pickup Lines for Female Pirates

10. That's quite a nine-incher ye've got thar. I'll bet I could set it off with one touch.
9. Is that a belayin' pin in yer breeches, or are ye . . . (She never gets to finish this one, because the guy always blurts out "Yes, I'm happy to see you!" Always.)
8. Come show me how ye bury yer treasure, lad!
7. Ye know, I've never met a man with a real yardarm before.
6. I can see yer mizzenmast is in need of buffin'!
5. Do ye fancy a climb in me rigging, matey?

4. I've crushed seventeen men's skulls between me thighs!
3. C'mon, lad, shiver me timbers!
2. RAMMING SPEED!
1. You. Pants. Off. Now!

Top Ten Pickup Lines for Gay and Lesbian Pirates

10. Toss me a line, come aboard, and I'll pull yer tender behind.
9. Wanna take a trip to the "Isle of Streisand"?
8. It be your choice—the cuddle or the cat-o'-nine-tails!
7. Want to see why they call me "saucy"?
6. I find the whole idea of sexual stereotyping almost as offensive as your juvenile attempt at sex-based humor! Do you want to have sex or not?
5. Say, ye're one gunner's daughter I'd like a taste of!
4. May I slip me monkey pump in yer bunghole?
3. Do you want to know what the Isle of Lesbos and I have in common? We both rely on the protection of Greece.
2. The story of the Dutch boy who put his finger in the dike has only two serious flaws . . .
1. You put the "arrr" in "homoARRRrotic"!

QUIZ

1. Why, as Max observed, are girls hard to catch? Is it fair? Do you know any guys who have

Corsair— Another name for "pirate," more often, we think, applied to the pirates of the Barbary Coast of "shores of Tripoli" fame than the classic Caribbean pirate, but still, a pirate all the same. Additionally, there are boats, airplanes and computer components that bear the CORSAIR insignia.

more than their fair share of success? Class project: Find those guys and beat them up.

2. Ol' Chumbucket took a cooking class to meet girls. Cap'n Slappy prefers to get them "all drunk and kissy." Of the two, which one do you think is in a long-term, happy marriage with a wonderful family, and which is a drunken lonely bastard who prays nightly for the sweet release of merciful death?
3. The top ten lists in this chapter were developed by the Pirate Guys in order to attract the producers of late-night television shows. What media appearance do you think is more likely?
   a) An interview with Katie Couric on NBC's *Today Show*
   b) A witty chat with TV's Ellen DeGeneres
   c) A Guinness-infused conversation with the hosts of *Good Morning, Galway*
   d) A walk-on appearance on perennial cable access favorite, *Weird Shit with Tom and Doug*
4. Do women really prefer a sense of humor to a stud muffin? Really? Sure, they say that now, but where were they back in high school when we were looking for prom dates? Seriously, we want names!
5. How important is hygiene to you when assessing potential partners for either long-term or one-night relationships? Have you considered lowering your standards? Have you considered HAVING standards?

7

Dress for Excess: Fashion and the Pirate Guys

In Which the Pirate Guys offer tips on how to dress with pirattitude and, like a fool, you take their advice.

An Unexpected Bonus

John's daughter Alex was home from college and he was excitedly showing her his new acquisition, a replica flintlock dueling pistol. "How much did that cost?" she asked.

"Not much," he replied. "Not as much as my sword."

Then, with great pride, he pulled out his new tricorn hat. "Okay," he said, "I paid too much for that. But the guy knocked ten bucks off the price just because I'm Ol' Chumbucket! How could I turn it down?"

Alex looked at John with bemusement for a moment, then said, "You know, a lot of my friends' dads are having really destructive midlife crises, so I guess this is okay."

Clothes make the man, the old saying goes, and that's no less true for pirates than anyone else. We have noticed a definite correlation between personality type and career choice on the one hand and personal toggery on the other.

So let's give a look at what the well-dressed pirate guy is wearing this season—or any season, because guys tend not to be influenced as much by the fickle winds of fashion as others. In fact, real pirates tended to wear the same clothes day in and day out, year in and year out, cleaned only by the occasional keelhauling. This may, in part, explain the phenomenon researchers call "that funky pirate smell."

Anyone who has seen our picture and STILL

turns to us for fashion advice probably deserves what he gets. But at least you can't say you haven't been warned.

Stede Bonnet
Rating: The worst pirate ever
Reputation: Whiny
Talent: None
Buckle: Totally unswashed
Why would a retired army officer, a rich plantation owner of Barbados, toss it all aside for a life at sea as a pirate? Legend says he fled a nagging wife. His neighbors assumed he was crazy. Either way, it was a poor career choice. After some initial, if minor success he fell in with Blackbeard, who quickly saw that he was no seaman and took over his ship. As a "guest" of Blackbeard, Bonnet got all weepy and vowed to give up piracy. He took a king's pardon, but no sooner had it been granted than he was back at sea under an assumed name. He was captured by a Captain Rhett, who knew him, so the jig was up. He cut such a pathetic figure that many citizens, even Captain Rhett, asked the governor to spare his life. But not even his own tear-stained appeal could save him, and Stede Bonnet was hanged in 1718.

To the Wenches

This is a fashion guide from guys to guys, in the broadest sense of the word "guy," which can include women. ("Hey guys!" you shout as you walk into a room of men and women. Admit it, you do too!) But remember, as ill-prepared as we are to offer fashion tips to men, we are at least doubly inadequate as grooming advisors to women. So the best we can offer in addition to the information in this chapter (and disregarding the whole "boxers or briefs" discussion) is this mantra—Go Sexy, Go Saucy and Be Ever-So-Lusty! In fact, Cap'n Slappy has those very words tattooed on his left forearm.

Shy modesty is fine for convent school, but if you are the pirate guy we think you are, young lady, you'll announce your presence with authority and cartoonlike force, causing eyeballs to pop from their sockets on humorous-sounding springs. (BOING!) You get the picture.

Let's Get This out of the Way: Boxers or Briefs?

Once upon a time, this was the sort of question you would NEVER hear asked. It just wasn't anybody else's business. As a boy growing up, you

Dos and Don'ts

If ye want to announce yer presence with authority, then ye've got to adhere to the following Pirate Fashion Dos and Don'ts.

Headwear

Do: Wear a weather-resistant tricorn hat (plumage optional).

Don't: Wear a baseball cap that sports a suspicious white blotch and the words "Damn Seagulls!" Not that funny.

Do: Wear a head scarf tied off at the back of the head that flaps heroically in the wind.

Don't: Wear a shower cap covered with humorously drawn cartoon duckies.

Do: Wear large gold earrings that denote your sailing experience and provide payment for your inevitable funerary expenses.

Don't: Wear that earring in your nose. It's an EAR-ring, for gawd's sake! And don't sport dangly "cascading pearl drop" earrings even though they do look fabulous and make your face and neck appear to be thinner.

Do: Wear an eye patch either to cover up an ocular cavity or over a perfectly good eye just to look dashing.

Don't: Wear X-ray glasses that you ordered out of a comic book. They don't work and they make you look gullible.

Above the Waist

Do: Wear your pirate bling-bling. Beads, medallions, rum tots and flower leis are all a part of your masculine femininity. (Feminine masculinity?)

Don't: Wear a dead albatross around your neck. You

wouldn't think we'd have to say this, but some people just need reminding.

Do: Wear a blousy shirt with puffy sleeves and show plenty of chest!

Don't: Wear an "I'm With Stupid" T-shirt. It wasn't funny twenty-eight years ago and it still isn't.

Do: Wear a colorful sash in which you may keep many weapons handy.

Don't: Wear rainbow suspenders bestrewn with Ziggy buttons imparting Life's Little Lessons.

Breeches and Boots

Do: Wear your breeches either skintight or baggy as an elephant's skin (depending on your youth and body type).

Don't: Wear a sundress. We don't care how beautiful the weather is or how liberating it feels. Do not do this if you're a guy, even if you have the legs for it. It's just not piratical. However, wenches should feel more than welcome to sport such gear. It gets sunny aboard ship.

Do: Wear a kilt to celebrate your Celtic heritage.

Don't: Wear lederhosen to celebrate your Bavarian heritage.

Do: Wear long leather boots to protect your legs from the elements as well as in battle.

Don't: Mortgage your home or raid your kid's college fund just to buy a pair of long leather boots. Also, do not wear oversized clown shoes no matter how many laughs it gets from the lads.

Do: Keep a boot knife tucked away in your boot in the event of close-quarter fighting.

Don't: Keep a sardine sandwich in your pants in the event of closed-galley snacking.

Crow's nest— A platform, sometimes enclosed, at the highest point of a ship, on which a lookout or two would perch. In your case, pretty much anytime you're going to go upstairs or to the restroom (it works either way), you might say you're going to visit the crow's nest. And as you leave the restroom, you might tell the next person taking a *shift* to "look out."

wore the underwear your mother handed you, and you wouldn't dream of discussing it with her. We have absolutely no idea why our mothers chose for us the underwear they did, and we don't want to know. In all probability, that's the kind of underwear you still wear today. In fact, considering how attached guys can become to their old underwear, you might still be wearing skivvies your mom bought you twenty or more years ago. Better check the label.

But in these new, modern, a-go-go times, everything is out in the open, including underwear—literally. It even became a matter of national policy when an MTV audience asked presidential candidate Clinton the B-or-B question. Instead of suggesting to the young inquisitor that it really wasn't an appropriate thing to ask a presidential candidate and that there were more pressing issues to consider, he answered. We can't recall what his answer was, but the fact that he just up and answered struck us at the time as the nadir of our civilization. We've seen a lot more since.

And of course, complicating the question is the proliferation of styles of underwear. Back when we were young pirates with stars in our eyes, there were boxers and there were briefs and that was that. Now there are all kinds of choices—bikini, European pouches that look like slingshots and—sweet sassy molassy!—thongs! Even mesh novelty underwear for those special occasions. There are mail-order catalogs devoted entirely to men's underwear! It boggles the mind.

So let's leave it at that simple question: Do

Pirate Guys wear boxers, or do they wear briefs? And the answer is, yes. You'll notice that there are two of us. One of us prefers the roominess and comfort—what he calls the "dangleisciousness"—of boxers with enough room to rent out space to a Bulgarian family. The other feels more comfortable with the added support in this vital region where a slip can mean disaster. But we're not going to say who is who. All you can do is look at our picture in the back of this book and try to guess, and if that mental image blinds your mind's eye, well, it serves you right.

So You Want to Dress Like a Pirate? Okay, but Why?

We used to get asked a lot, "You're the Pirate Guys. Why don't you dress like pirates?" Well, there was a good reason for that. It's a lot of work. We have nothing AGAINST anyone dressing like pirates, but it just seemed like a lot of bother to us. The fun, for us, is in TALKING like a pirate, and getting the rest of the world to join us every September 19.

But as the enthusiasm for the holiday grew and we got more and more requests for interviews and appearances, we realized we would have to bow to expectations. We are the Pirate Guys, and now we dress the part.

It is fun, we have to admit. How often do you get to wear a sword in your average daily life? And write its cost off on your taxes! See? It's cool!

A Quick and Dirty Guide to Pirate Drag

1. A little black eye patch goes a long, long way.
2. If you have a pierced ear, a big thick gold hoop is very helpful. But not too big. This isn't Talk Like Liberace Day.
3. If you don't want to go to the trouble and expense of tracking down a good quality tricorn hat, a bandana tied around the head is a much easier alternative. Black would be the best color. Red will work in a pinch. DO NOT go for the train-engineer pattern that you find almost everywhere. Solid color. Cut up a sheet if you have to, especially if your head is that extra capacious size that signifies large brains and drives the girls wild. Again, check our picture.
4. A loose shirt of the type known as a "poet's blouse" (and we can't believe we just used the word "blouse," but we ARE talking about Pirate Drag here) is important. You can pretty much forget about the pants and shoes if you have the right shirt, perhaps with lacing at the neck instead of buttons. White or black. If you can't find (or, more likely, don't want to go to the trouble of finding) a proper shirt, you might try taking an old white dress shirt from a considerably larger friend or uncle and removing

Putting on what we call "pirate drag" gives you permission to act outrageously, and not only do onlookers allow you to, they enjoy it! They get into the fun of having pirates raiding their party. We find ourselves in restaurants, plopping down in a booth and asking the startled patrons, "Well, the collar and sleeves. Frankly, we don't know what this would signify, but we've found that if you've gone to that much trouble, people will just assume you know what you're doing. A sash completes the effect.

5. If money is no object, go out and get yourself a pair of knee-high (or higher) leather boots, preferably with a big (three inches or more) cuff. As for us, we have house payments to make, kids to put through college, and wenches to woo with our ill-gotten booty, so that's not high on the list. But a really impressive pair of boots will negate any need to do something special with the pants. If you can't get the boots (and who can?) we'd go with black dress slacks. You might want to distress them so that it looks like you live in them at sea, amid battles and pillaging and chum spills and deprivations of all kinds. Or, if you're a typical guy, your pants have been distressed by day-to-day living and spilling of food, so you're already ahead of the game there.
6. If you really want to cement the look, and don't mind a fair amount of discomfort, try to figure out a peg leg or a hook for your hand. The advantage would be that then you would only need one boot, presumably cutting down the cost.

what are we eatin' today?"—then picking at their plates for a few minutes before getting up and annoying someone else. Except mostly they're not annoyed. They love it!

Strapping on a cutlass and stuffing a pistol in your sash may be the coolest thing you'll ever do.

Freebooter— Yet another word for "pirate." Also, a good price for footwear.

Cutlass— The weapon of choice among pirates. A cutlass is a short, heavy, curved sword with a single edge. When fighting in the confined space of a ship's deck, you didn't want a long rapier or broadsword, because your weapon could easily get caught in the rigging. A cutlass does the job.

But the garb becomes your work clothes, after a while, not all that different than the dorky paper hat the kid at the fast-food restaurant puts on to cover his hairnet. It's the uniform of our job.

Still, we have to say it's a great job.

The Pirate Guy on the Town

Depending on your circle of friends, pirate drag can be suitable for almost any occasion. Our friends, who happen to mostly be theater folk, wouldn't even blink if we walked into the room dressed like a pair of guys fresh from a brisk swash of their buckles. But you might hang with a different crowd—your city-league softball team, for instance, or the guys at the garage, or the hip, trendy young crowd at the hip, trendy new clubs. (We haven't hung out at such a club since people actually used the words "trendy" and "hip.") Or you might be a powerful, politically connected attorney who hangs out at the golf course with people named Thad and J.P., but we doubt it, because you wouldn't be reading our book if you were. You would normally read the *Wall Street Journal* or *Country Club Lawyers at Play* magazine.

If any of those are the case, you should wear the appropriate uniform, whether it's sweats, or grease-stained T-shirts, or the latest hip fashions, or a hideously expensive three-piece suit, and save the pirate outfit for a few special occasions, such as costume parties, bachelor parties, and appearances before the Ninth Circuit Court of Appeals. ("May it please the court, Arrrr!")

Our advice for dressing for work and play is what pretty much any guy would tell you: Go for comfort. There's no point in being pinched by a tight collar and tie if the conditional rigors of your job don't require it. So our look is usually some rumpled sports clothes pulled from the closet, with the color scheme based less on fashion than what's present and relatively clean. A loose-fitting shirt, loose-fitting breeches, a baggy sweater, running shoes (not that we run that much, but you know). It's a look that makes a statement, and the statement is, "I'm not dressing to make anyone happy but myself. You never know when I may have to spring into action. I wouldn't want to be restricted by the grip of too-tight clothing!"

Ties: The Hempen Halter

The hempen halter is, of course, the pirate phrase that means the noose around the neck of a hanged man, which seems to us the appropriate analogy for a tie. If your job requires you to wear a tie five days a week you have our sympathy. If you wear a tie every day because you actually like them, you have our vote for Dork of the Year.

Several years ago John made a New Year's resolution to not wear a tie for a full year. His wife commented at the time, "You need better problems." But it was the first resolution he ever made

Dance the hempen jig— Dangle from the end of a hangman's noose. We recommend that you NOT wear dancing shoes—they'll just get jerked off when you come to the end of your hemp.

that he actually kept for a full year. He liked it so much he made it again the next year, and has hardly ever worn a tie since. Like McNamara's Band, his ties come out only for wakes and weddings and every fancy ball.

Ties can be tasteful, but what fun is that? The uglier and louder the better, we say. If you have to wear one, wear one that says, "Look at me! I'm the one he actually dared to take out of the closet. Change the tie rule or he'll wear the REALLY ugly one." This is the passive-aggressive rule of tie wearing: Purchase ties so ugly as to hold your clients, your co-workers and your boss visually hostage.

We would just close this section with the observation that no one really HAS to wear a tie anymore. Our shirts all come with the collars sewn right on. That's what ties were for, of course, to attach your collar to your shirt. But it's been a long time since we've seen collarless shirts and celluloid collars down at the mercantile, so ties are pretty much obsolete.

QUICK QUIZ

1. Based on photos I've seen of the Pirate Guys, I would:
   a) not take their fashion advice
   b) be uneasy sharing a sidewalk with them
   c) move if they lived in my neighborhood
   d) follow their advice slavishly, since they still dress better than I do

2. True or false: The Pirate Guys' circle of theater friends sounds more interesting than the people I hang out with. Follow-up question: If I had a sister who was really hot, would I sacrifice her maidenly chastity to Cap'n Slappy's unspeakably heathen carnal lust in order to hang out with them? (For those who answered yes, send a phone number and your sister's photo and we'll get back to you. Operators are standing by!)
3. Have you ever used the words "hip" or "trendy"? How embarrassed are you about that now?
4. If *Country Club Lawyers at Play* were a real magazine, would you subscribe to it? Why or why not?
5. My favorite tie is decorated with:
   a) stripes
   b) polka dots
   c) cartoon characters
   d) gravy

8

Then and Now: Comparing Pirates and Players

In Which the Pirate Guys demonstrate that you may already be flaunting pirattitude.

Much of what we do and wear these days has a link to our pirate heritage.

Well, no, wait. We have to admit that's not strictly true. A lot of what we do and wear these days has no connection whatsoever with our pirate heritage. Hardly anything. But that's not going to stop us from counterfeiting a link, just for the fun of it.

Pirates

Jolly Roger—Shows yer loyalty to yer mates and delight in pillagin'.

Tricorn hat—Shields yer head from the weather.

Eye patch—Protects empty eye socket from salt water and spares others the nauseating sight of your ocular disfigurement.

Large earring—Shows that you can at least afford your own funeral.

Scabbard—Keeps "tools of the trade" available for ready use.

Cutlass/Pistol/Dagger—"Tools of the trade" that build your fortunes and destroy the lives of others. Size matters: the bigger the better.

Breeches—Worn to emphasize one's legs and genitals.

Knee-length boots—Footwear designed to get one from place to place with style.

Today

Nike logo—Shows loyalty to a brand name and yer delight in chillin' at the mall.

Ball cap—Shields bad hair days from your co-workers.

Sunglasses—Protect eyes from dangerous ultraviolet rays and spares others the humorous sight of your lazy eye.

Small ear stud—Shows that you can at least pretend to be a rebel.

Pocket protector—Keeps "tools of the trade" available for ready use.

Mechanical Pencil/Pen/Cell Phone—Yeah, pretty much the same. Size matters: the smaller the better.

Trousers—Worn to conceal one's legs and genitals.

Cross-trainers—Footwear designed to get one from place to place with speed.

Davy Jones' locker—The bottom of the sea, specifically the watery grave of drowning victims. Why Davy Jones? You will read occasionally someone claiming authoritatively that it refers to this person or that, but the fact is no one really knows. If you listen silently over the stillness of the water, you may occasionally catch the refrain from the Monkees hit "Daydream Believer."

QUICK QUIZ

1. Is a pocket protector really equivalent to a sword's scabbard, or were the authors just making another of their little "jokes"? If it is, how cool is that?
2. What are the odds that Nike will sue the authors for using their name in this book? Really? That bad? Hmmm.
3. True or false: If you could get away with it, you would love to get rid of your belt and wear a sash every day.
4. If a brace of pistols beats a full house, what poker hand beats a cannon loaded with grapeshot and rusty nails?
5. And speaking of footwear, on a scale of one to ten, one being a field of lilacs after a light spring shower and ten being a festering bucket of pig turds in a cauldron full of boiling sulfur, how bad do your feet smell at the end of the day?

9

You Can't Spell Pirate Without Ate, or Pie, or the Letter R

In Which the Pirate Guys help you make your way in the ship's galley.

Dining on a real pirate ship in the Golden Age of piracy, from roughly the sixteenth into the nineteenth century, was probably not the greatest culinary experience on the planet.

Even the nicer pirate ships, the *Whydah*, the *Mocha Frigate* and the

Deadlights— Eyes. Not sure where this one came from, but we like it a lot. "Damn yer deadlights," you might say as your friend beats you in yet another game of darts. This should never be confused with "headlights," which one might find on a particularly buxom wench. Or, as Cementhands McCormack is fond of calling them, "upper frontals."

Queen Anne's Revenge, were not the *Queen Mary*. There was a noticeable dearth of gourmet chefs with five-star kitchens at sea. This was NOT the *Love Boat*, and Blackbeard never pretended to be Julie, your cruise director. Life at sea was hard, and so was most of the food. The first concern of the ship's quartermaster and cook was how long the food could be stored without going rancid, not how to whip up an airy soufflé or other fancy meal that would satisfy the most finicky member of the crew. Picky eaters were out of luck.

So the real fare of a pirate ship—or really, most ships of the day—tended to be dry and heavily salted, stored in barrels for months at a time. You think they were eating hardtack and pickles and salted beef because it was their favorite? No, they ate it because it was filling and could be counted on to last a long sea voyage.

Cap'n Slappy and Ol' Chumbucket are not historians or pirate reenactors. We're not even real people! We're the pirate personas of your authors, Mark and John, two fairly normal guys who venture into the kitchen only as a matter of survival. And as we've mentioned before, our research tends to be a tad on the casual side, so when you ask us, "What do pirates eat?" we generally answer, "Something not really that good." But if you ask us, "What do the Pirate Guys eat?" we'd be happy to tell you, because we are in fact the Pirate Guys.

The Perfect Food

Whenever we want to dine in pirate style, the number one thing on our menu is barbecued pork ribs. Not because we love them, although we do. And not only because the way to eat them (grip rib in hand, tear meat off with teeth, snarl) is appropriately barbaric, although it is.

Barbecued pork ribs are the most piratically appropriate food for the day for thoroughly historical reasons.

The word "buccaneer" comes from the French word *boucanier,* literally meaning "eater of wild pork." It's kind of a long story, but here goes. The Spanish wanted the Western Hemisphere to themselves. (Yes, we know there were already people living here when Columbus got here. Complain to the Spanish, not us.) The Spanish had a tendency to kill any non-Spanish colonists they found in the New World. They attacked foreign settlers in the Caribbean, first French and then Dutch, English and—who knows—Canadian and Czechoslovakian? These undesirables lived in isolation and subsisted mostly on wild pigs that lived on the islands. They became really good at chasing them down, catching them and killing them with knives, rarely having to resort to shooting them.

The meat was cut into strips and laid on a grating of green wood called a *barbecu* (from which comes our word "barbecue," but you'd already guessed that, you clever thing, you) above a slow-burning fire, and was cured by the heat and smoke. The cured meat was called *boucan*. The people who

Bartholomew Roberts
Nickname: Black Bart Roberts
Rating: Best pirate of the Golden Age
Call him the Reluctant Pirate, since he was an honest seaman captured by pirates and forced to go on the account. Call him the Dry Pirate, since he didn't drink and tried to keep his crew from doing so. Call him Popeye the Sailor Man, for all we care. Just make sure you call him the most successful pirate of the Golden Age, possibly in history. He was captured by pirates in 1719. He was soon elected captain. Within two years he had taken close to 400 ships and more than 51 million pounds worth of treasure, single-handedly bringing to a virtual halt all Spanish shipping in the Caribbean. He then pillaged the African coast with equal success until running into a British naval patrol in 1722. In combat with the HMS *Swallow* (yes, there's a joke there), he was killed in the cannonading. To prevent his body being taken, the crew tossed his remains overboard before being captured themselves.

Deck— Technically this is the part of the ship you stand on. But you're not on a ship. There's a good probability the biggest ship you've ever been on was a canoe back at Boy Scout camp when you were a kid. For your purposes, the deck is the floor, because any sea dog worth his salt would never call any floor anything other than a deck. And, typically, the thing you do with the deck is swab it. You may also be directed to "hit" the deck.

ate *boucan* became known as buccaneers. And today's stereotypical American barbecuer, with his gas grill and chrome cooking tools and novelty apron with humorous sayings or comically exaggerated genitalia, is the modern version of those happy hunters.

The Spanish left them alone for a while (the buccaneers, not the moderns), but eventually decided they constituted a menace that had to be driven out. They tried killing off the wild game on which the buccaneers lived, but realized it would be easier just to kill off the buccaneers. This naturally did not endear the Spanish to the buccaneers and made the latter easily recruited by the English for privateering. The early buccaneers did not often raid English shipping. On the whole they found a broader and more profitable lifestyle on the open seas preying on Spanish treasure ships than they had chasing pigs on an island.

The last time we checked the meat department at Safeway there was no wild pig to be had. So we're improvising here. Pork spareribs take the place of strips of wild pork, but the barbecue remains the same.

Come to think of it, a nice bacon, lettuce and tomato sandwich would work in a pinch, especially if the tomatoes are fresh.

A Little of Everything—or a Lot

If you want to go to some trouble and shoot for real authenticity (and God knows why you'd want to do THAT) you could rustle up a salmagundi. This was a delicacy on a pirate ship, a pirate favorite. A salmagundi is a dish of chopped meat, eggs, anchovies, onions and perhaps whatever else was lying around aboard ship. The word has come to refer to any assortment or medley of ingredients. Again, this is the twenty-first century, not the seventeenth, so we have to improvise. We have a recipe below for an actual, honest to God salmagundi, but we don't recommend anyone go to that kind of trouble. Instead, focus on the second half of the definition, the "assembly or medley." Order a large pizza with everything. We mean EVERYTHING. And call it a salmagundi pie. Heck, you might even convince the pizzeria owner to adopt that as the name for a giant pizza with everything.

But if you really want to go for it, here's a recipe, taken from a cookbook published in 1747.

Take two or three Roman or Cabbage Lettice, and when you have washed them clean, swing them pretty dry in a Cloth; then beginning at the open End, cut them cross-ways, as fine as a good big Thread, and lay the Lettices so cut, about an Inch thick all over the Bottom of the Dish.

When you have thus garnished your Dish, take a Couple of cold roasted Pullets, or Chickens, and cut the Flesh off the Breasts and Wings into Slices, about three Inches long, a Quarter of an Inch broad, and as thin as a Shilling; lay them upon the Lettice round the End to the Middle of the Dish and the other towards the Brim; then

Due to an editing mix-up, the scoring guide for the Pi-Q has been moved to page 139 for safekeeping. Please find it there and follow the instructions carefully.

Take a caulk— Rest. The spaces between planks of a deck were caulked, or filled with a putty or tar, to keep them watertight. Just like today's tourist aboard a Carnival cruise ship, pirates liked to stretch out in the sun when they had some free time and nap on the deck. Unlike Carnival cruisers, they would often get lines of caulk on their backs.

having boned and cut six Anchovies each into eight Pieces, lay them all between each Slice of the Fowls, then cut the lean Meat of the Legs into Dice, and cut a Lemon into small Dice; then mince the Yolks of four Eggs, three or four Anchovies, and a little Parsley, and make a round Heap of these in your Dish, piling it up in the Form of a Sugar-loaf, and garnish it with Onions, as big as the Yolk of Eggs, boiled in a good deal of Water very tender and white.

Put the largest of the Onions in the Middle on the Top of the Salamongundy, and lay the rest all round the Brim of the Dish, as thick as you can lay them; then beat some Sallat-Oil up with Vinegar, Salt and Pepper and pour over it all. Garnish with Grapes just scalded, or French beans blanched, or Station [nasturtium] Flowers, and serve it up for a first Course.

[FROM HANNAH GLASSE, *THE ART OF COOKERY* . . . 1747, PP. 59–60]

Sounds like a lot of trouble for what amounts to an antipasto, doesn't it? We say, either order the cold-cut tray from your local deli, or go with our pizza idea.

For dessert? We suppose some kind of dessert based on citrus fruit would be good, to fight scurvy. Lime sherbet, anyone? It's one of our favorites.

What Shall We Drink?

Beer, you fool! Lots and lots of beer!

Well, of course, this only applies to those who are of legal drinking age. If you're younger than twenty-one, we remind you that alcohol is terrible stuff. It's dangerous and it can ruin your life. Oh, no, youngsters, stay away from the beer. One of the most famous pirates of all, Black Bart Roberts, was a teetotaler whose rules forbade the consumption of alcohol aboard ship. We don't want to minimize the dangers of alcohol abuse, so any of you of any age who have issues about this should just jump ahead and read the chapter on parties. That's a good sport . . . Are they gone? Good. Let's talk about beer.

Forget what we said to the kids. That was just us trying to be good parents. Beer is the elixir of life, the magic mixture of hops and grains that does so much to justify God's ways to man, or at least explain man's ways to God. It inspires the articulation of genuine guy affection—like that time your best friend said, "Dude. You know something, dude? You and me, dude. Dude." Good times.

For those of you who enjoy the well-known massively marketed tasteless national brands, that's certainly your prerogative and we wish you well.

Grog—A Very Incomplete Timeline

Dawn of time—Humans need liquid during sea voyages. Water was stored in barrels, which over time became alarmingly green and slimy. A solution was needed to keep the water palatable. Primitive man tried many methods to preserve it, including adding rocks, adding salt and adding water. (Hey, we said he was primitive.) Even more alarming, beer stored aboard the ship often went sour. Something had to be done.

1655—British vice admiral William Penn arrived in Barbados and captured Jamaica. Jamaica had few stores of beer or wine but it did have quite a bit of rum. Penn began to use it as a ration. As the popularity of Jamaica as a port of call increased, the use of rum spread widely until it was common aboard ships of all nationalities. This period was known as "the Golden Age," but all of its friends called it "Ol' Rummy."

1731—Rum became an official part of the British Navy's "Regulations and Instructions Relating to His Majesty's Service at Sea." Under the rules, a half pint of undiluted rum was equal to the provision of a gallon of beer. Personally, we'd go for the beer, but we're not picky.

1740—British vice admiral Edward Vernon had to deal with a problem becoming more common aboard ship—sailors who became drunk and disorderly after their evening ration. On August 21, 1740, Vernon issued an order that rum would thereafter be mixed with water. This was the invention of the cocktail. The order earned him several nicknames, among them Admiral Buzz-kill, Sir Mix-a-lot and Auntie Vern. A quart of water was mixed with a half pint of rum on deck and in the presence of the lieutenant of the watch. Sailors were given two servings a day: between ten and twelve a.m. and between four and six p.m. To make it more palatable it was suggested sugar and lime be added. In 1756 the mixture of water and rum became part of the regulations, and the call to "up spirits" sounded aboard Royal Navy ships for more than two centuries thereafter.

1805—Lord Horatio Nelson, possibly the greatest fighting seaman ever, was killed at the Battle of Trafalgar, in which his fleet destroyed Napoleon's navy. Nelson's body was put in a barrel of rum to preserve it on the long voyage home. (As a nobleman and national hero he couldn't be buried at sea, so he was respectfully pickled instead. By the way, we don't know if this is where the phrase "getting pickled" for getting drunk came from, but it seems reasonable.) According to the legend, sailors aboard the ship snuck drinks of the rum in the cask, not knowing that the admiral was in there as well. From that day on rum has been known as "Nelson's Blood."

1823—The beginning of the end. Diluting the rum with water didn't cure the problem of drunkenness. That's still a lot of rum to be drinking. In 1823 the Admiralty cut the daily grog ration in half, to one quarter pint (one gill). In return, sailors were issued tea and cocoa, an extra two shillings a month and an increased meat ration. This became known as "the Sissy Age" of seafaring.

1850—The Admiralty's Grog Committee released a report blaming discipline problems on grog and recommended the ration be eliminated. The Admiralty was afraid to go that far, knowing how jealous the sailors were of their privilege, so effective January 1, 1851, the ration was decreased to a half gill, or one eighth of a pint. This decision led to "the Misguided Rebellion," in which a group of sailors took their entire ship's store of rum and dumped it in the sea chanting "Half a gill will never thrill!" When the captain pointed out that "something is better than nothing," the Misguided Rebellion was squelched and replaced immediately by the Regretful Malaise.

1862—The American Navy ends the grog ration. The British Navy was not so quick to bow to political correctness.

1970—The Great Rum Debate took place in the House of Commons on January 28, and July 30, 1970, became "Black Tot Day," the last pipe of "up spirits" in the Royal Navy. Since then, the greatness* of the British Navy has been restored.

*Greatness limited to the Outer Hebrides and the Falkland Islands.

We will never say anything bad about one of those outfits or their beer, mostly because we haven't completely abandoned hope that one of them will hire us to be national spokesmen for an enormous sum of money and we'll never have to work again (as if writing this is particularly hard work).

But in the meantime, we'd just point out the many, many fine beers made by the country's growing army of craft brewers (God bless 'em all). From the four corners of this great country—from Maine (Black Fly Stout) to San Diego (Arrogant Bastard Ale), from Florida (Hurricane Reef and Gaspar's Ale) to the Pacific Northwest (Dead Guy

Ale, Steelhead), there is a veritable bevy of fine, craft-brewed beers and no reason to drink tasteless beer unless that's what you actually want. Or unless you're in Mason City, Iowa, where Ol' Chumbucket spent one of the longest nights of his life, moving from bar to bar in a futile effort to find a dark beer. They looked at him as if he were insane—but they'd been looking at him that way during the day's business meetings as well, so maybe it wasn't the beer.

Rum-based drinks are always appropriate for the holiday as well, because of their Caribbean connection. And gin and tonic is always a good choice for a pirate, since it has a slice of lime in it and that's good for fighting off scurvy.

Potent Potables

You really don't need a recipe for authentic grog. But if you're the sort of person who freezes in the kitchen without written instructions, try these.

Basic Grog

Rum
Water

Mix in glass. Adjust proportions to taste.

There are in fact many bar recipes for "grog" that resemble the simple concoction above, if at all, only in that they have rum in them. We've even

Doubloon— A Spanish gold coin. Worth two pistoles. Don't ask us what a pistole was worth. We'll say "half a doubloon." We also have no idea how strong it is against the yen.

had someone send us her personal recipe for "grog" that has more coffee in it than anything else. Having rum doesn't necessarily make a drink grog, although that's no reason to turn your nose up at it either. We'll pass on a few recipes that have been sent to us. We don't swear by them, but you might want to try one.

Or just drink the rum.

Dungbie— Rear end. Whether the ship's or a pirate's we have no idea. It's just a word we picked up somewhere and were told on relatively good authority that it's a pirate word. Sounds Scottish to us. "Ach! I'll be stayin' in Dungbie with the MacTavishes and their wee bairns!"

Grog 1

1 shot rum
1 teaspoon sugar
A dash of lime juice
Cinnamon stick
Boiling water

Stir all ingredients, adding enough boiling water to fill mug or glass.

Grog 2

½ oz light rum
½ oz gold rum
½ oz dark rum
½ oz Grand Marnier
1 oz pineapple juice
1 oz orange juice
1 oz grapefruit juice

Pour liquors into an ice-filled collins glass. Add juices, shake, and garnish with an orange wedge and pineapple chunk. Sounds like a lot of work to us.

Grog 3

2 fl oz rum
Boiling water
1 sugar lump
The juice of half an organic lemon
2 cloves
1 small stick of cinnamon

Put all the ingredients into a mug and fill with boiling water. If preferred, serve in a strong tumbler when the drink has cooled a little (so as not to break the glass).

QUICK QUIZ

1. At the beginning of this chapter the authors say they are not real people. True or false: This is the kind of conundrum that gives me a headache.
2. When barbecuing pork ribs, the sauce I cook with is:
   a) Heinz
   b) KC Masterpiece
   c) Sweet Baby Ray's
   d) Are you kidding? I don't use a bottled sauce! I use an old family recipe to mix up the sweetest, tangiest sauce you've ever laid lip to
   e) I make my own by adding ketchup to whatever sauce was cheapest at the store

Fathom— A unit of measurement that, in the days of the Caribbean pirates, tended to be somewhat flexible. It's about six feet, with the emphasis on "about." To measure a line, sailors of the time would grab it, extending it from the tip of the outstretched right hand to the tip of the outstretched left. One fathom. Imagine the difference in fathoms if your crew included, say, Shaquille O'Neal and Billy Barty.

3. Which sentence makes more sense?
   a) Salmagundi was a favorite dish aboard pirate ships.
   b) Sal Magundi played second base for the Pittsburgh Pirates in 1938.
4. Beer is:
   a) just wrong and bad
   b) the magic mixture of hops and grains
   c) both delicious AND nutritious
   d) your only real friend, the only thing that truly loves you
   e) all of the above
5. Is Nelson's Blood the coolest name you've ever heard for an alcoholic beverage? If not, what is? Would it be a good name for a band? We thought so, too.

10

Buccaneer Balls: Party Like It's 1699!

In Which you will learn how to throw a Talk Like a Pirate Day celebration that will be the social event of the season! And maybe stay out of jail.

Figurehead— The carved figure at the front of the ship. Vikings (and they were fine pirates, aye!) used dragons. The English preferred figures of women. The Chinese often painted eyes on the bows of their ships to help them see in the dark. The Japanese, of course, fashioned their figurehead in the form of a Pokémon—the one that looked like a marshmallow with pointy ears and whiskers.

Hey! How about a nice big party to celebrate Talk Like a Pirate Day every September 19? With games and drinking and stuff? How does THAT grab ye!?!

"But," you interject, "what sort of games would we play, and what would we drink? Whom should we invite and not invite, and what if your little holiday lands inconveniently on a weekday? And did I use 'whom' correctly?" (Yes, you did. Nice work, Poindexter).

You ask a lot of questions. But if you read on, we will try to answer them all—as well as some that we come up with along the way. In the meantime, please accept this celebratory blow to the head as a token of our disdain for you and your line of questioning.

The Invitations

The key to any important event is setting the right tone. Who you invite is of little importance to us—HOW you invite them is. We recommend taking high-grade white paper and soaking it in tea to give it that aged look, then burning the edges of the paper to create a "treasure map" feel. Sure, it sounds work-intensive, but if you just use your children—or our children; we'll rent them out to you—it will go quickly. Nothing warms our piratical hearts like the sight of six-year-olds with matches, lighting and blowing out the edges of tea-soaked paper. (Note: Let paper dry before letting the children burn the edges—it's just easier that way.)

We recommend the following script for your invitations, but feel free to make it your own.

Ahoy, me salty dogs and saucy wenches! In honor of International Talk Like a Pirate Day on September 19, (insert your real/pirate name(s) here) is/are pleased to invite ye to our wee Pirate Ball / Pirate Party / Festival De Piratas / Celebration of Pirattitiude!

The Particulars:

When: (may be a date other than September 19 for convenience of hangover recovery)

Whar: (and any other information yer invitee may need to know)

For those who are unfamiliar with how to make the most of pirate talk, dress and "pirattitude," we recommend you purchase a copy of the indispensable guide to all things pirate by the Pirate Guys (plug our book here and let people know that it makes a great gift. Thanks).

In fact, we recommend that you make this book required reading before any of your guests are allowed to attend the party. Seriously, if they admit that they did not read this book, we strongly suggest you give them a savage pummeling with your fists and forehead.

Dominique You
Born: Who knows?
Died: 1830
Worked: The Gulf of Mexico
Most often called: Hey, You!
Born Frederic Youx, he was Jean Laffite's most trusted lieutenant and may have been his brother, since the origins of both men are rather cloudy and it makes a better story. You is also believed by some to have been an artilleryman in the army of Napoleon. In any case, he proved handy with a cannon. When Laffite and his men sided with the United States and General Andrew Jackson against the British in the War of 1812, it was You who manned the guns, serving with distinction at the Battle of New Orleans, which would have been a pivotal battle for the young country if it hadn't happened a couple of months after the war technically ended.

Rum— The essential drink of pirates, and the basis of song and story. And, coincidentally, the liquor on which John first got drunk lo these many years ago. He hasn't been able to drink rum since, because of the visceral recollection of throwing it up later. But if Craig and Owen, twin brothers and John's high school classmates who served him that drink, are out there reading this, he still remembers you fondly for it.

Planning the Party

Now, there is nobody in the party planning community who has earned as much piratical prestige as Martha "Shawshank Deduction" Stewart. Her soirées were, by all accounts, "to die for," although during her incarceration her bashes were naturally curtailed. Now that she is out, she has wisely kept her parties "on the down low." Sadly, she has never invited the Pirate Guys—a fact that we find both irksome and evidence of her good breeding. Best of all, since she never invited us to a party, we feel no compunction about making her the butt of the joke all the way through this chapter.

Anyway, we have had to glean what we can from her television program while keeping our own salty *je ne sais* whatever! Basically, we made up what we think she'd have said, based on some five-year-old Kmart commercials we vaguely remember. We'll offer our Marthaesque suggestions with our gut-level pirattitude to help you plan and implement the most dangerous party of the year!

Martha suggests—Limit the number of guests to a number that your setting may comfortably accommodate.

The Pirate Guys add—To pare down the list, make your selections based on the wealth, attractiveness and gullibility of your guests, and remember that the more crowded the room is, the better the chance is that someone hot will end up in your lap.

Martha suggests—Create a festive atmosphere

with a nautical theme, using nothing but gold, silver and the skeletal remains of your financial counselor. Pinecones hot-glued to an anchor and spray-painted antique gold make a nice centerpiece.

The Pirate Guys say—Rent a fog machine and set it on "extreme London." Tell guests you did decorate—they just can't see it through all this damned fog!

Martha suggests—Spanish beads dangling in doorways are also a nice touch.

The Pirate Guys say—Tell the wenches that beads are "pirate mistletoe."

Martha suggests—Prepare a delicious rum cake with a festive mint garnish and lime wedges carved to resemble an English frigate.

The Pirate Guys say—Alright. Lose the mint. Suck the lime (to ward off scurvy) and follow up the rum cake with a nice chaser of—oh, say, RUM!

Martha suggests—Place a delicious tropical punch outside near your garden's water feature. Make sure the gardening staff has manicured the area nicely for the event. And encourage guests to make their "pirate wish" and drop a coin in your water feature.

The Pirate Guys say—Show your generous side to the staff and tell them to dress up as koi and collect all of the money tossed into the water feature. Whatever funds are brought in, give them a five-spot and tell them it was a 25 percent gratuity.

Martha suggests—Get that authentic pirate

Filibuster— Not solely an attempt to talk a bill to death in the halls of Congress. This word is yet another name for a pirate. Political folks celebrating Talk Like a Pirate Day should take note of this one.

Flying colors— Nothing to do with rainbows or anything like that. A ship's flag was its colors (or "colours," for those aboard an English ship). If you wanted to be identified, you'd pass another ship with your colors flying. Of course, pirate ships flew under the Jolly Roger, and might not want the other ship to know who they were until they got close. So they flew false colors.

look using nothing more than silk pajamas (or "pyjamas"), a contrasting scarf and a designer eye patch.

The Pirate Guys say—Get that authentic pirate smell by wearing the same pants for three months prior to the festivities.

Martha suggests—Live on the wild side of the sea by limiting your place settings to four forks, three spoons and only two knives.

The Pirate Guys say—Eschew all utensils and eat only with fingers—someone else's. We recommend comely wenches, but you may prefer a fancy lad.

Martha suggests—Help your guests get into the spirit of things with a nautically themed music presentation. I recommend a Celtic hymn of the sea sung by your special guest entertainer, Enya.

The Pirate Guys say—For the love o' God, Martha! Not Enya again! How about some saucy songs of lust and disease by our ol' pals, Cap'n Bogg and Salty?

Martha suggests—Three words: Loganberry jellyfish compote!

The Pirate Guys say—Three other words: What the hell?

Martha suggests—Make sure there's plenty of fine wine available. I recommend wine that costs enough per bottle to send a kid through a year and a half of college.

The Pirate Guys say—Boxed wines are easy to stack and store, and don't fall over so much when the ship's caught in a gale.

Martha suggests—For that added whimsical touch, give each guest an individualized "treasure map" which will guide them to the same sitting room. At the gathering, point out to them that they are ALL a treasure.

The Pirate Guys say—How's this for a whimsical touch? Everyone drop your money and jewelry into this bag marked SWAG and I will donate it to a worthy charity—Cap'n Slappy's Home for Young Chumbucketeers.

The Games

Just as Dasher, Dancer, Prancer and their buddies had their reindeer games, so, too, did Blackbeard, Jack Rackham, Captain Blood and the crew have their pirate games. Our crack research and development team has taken a close look at traditional pirate games and, after consulting with our lawyers, we have decided not to mention them to you, because we don't want the liability. Instead, we offer a few modernized games that should reduce the number of limbs lost per party. Remember, if you can't play rough like a pirate, at least bring a bit of pirattitude to the party. Otherwise, you might as well put on a nice pointy hat and blow on a little noisemaker, breaking only occasionally to pin a paper tail on a picture of a donkey—whoopee!

The following is a list of games that may or may not be a bit too rough for a felony-free party. Just

Foc's'le— The dictionary calls it "a variant of forecastle." We call it one of our very favorite nautical words, if for no other reason than it's hard to say and hard to understand if you're not a mariner. It's "the section of the upper deck of a ship located at the bow forward of the foremast." If you're on a ship, you'll know you're at the foc's'le when you see some kid standing there with his fists in the air, yelling, "I'm the king of the world!" You could use it to describe the front section of whatever bar you're stopping in. "I'm the king of the bar!"

remember, these games are hideously dangerous and the insane decision to include them in your party is entirely yours, so don't even bother sending the subpoena.

Hack-n-Slash—A group of seven or eight combatants armed with short swords stand in a roped circle ten feet in diameter. A referee outside the circle yells, "Commence carnage," and the cutting begins. The winner is determined by whoever has been able to keep the highest percentage of his or her body parts INSIDE the circle after four minutes. Wacky rule: You don't need to remain alive to be declared the winner!

Bury the Booty—One person is selected to be It through the time-honored "eenie, meenie, meinie, mo" tradition. It is allowed to select one "treasure" item with which to be buried and is immediately interred in a wooden box (a crate will do) in a six-foot-deep hole which It will be tearfully forced to dig. IMPORTANT: The "treasure" item may NOT be a digging tool (exception: dynamite). If It manages to extricate Itself from certain death before the end of the party, It gets a piece of candy. Wacky rule: It may not use Its left hand.

Stick the Dagger in the Spanish Naval Officer—If you thought pin the tail on the donkey was fun, try this pirate adult version on for size. Build an effigy of a Spanish naval officer (if effigies are hard to come by in your area, a real Spanish naval officer will do) and hang it from a rope so its height can be quickly adjusted. The player is supplied with one or two eye patches (depending on the number of preexisting eye patches) and given a dagger. After the rest of the partygoers spin and pummel him for a minute or two (the pummeling will help the contestant focus, and is just fun for the rest of the guests) he will have five seconds to stick the dagger into the Spanish naval officer. The winner will be the person with the most humorously positioned dagger. Wacky rule: Every third player may be stripped naked and covered in vegetable oil before competing.

Of course, there are some newer, less violent piratical games that could be just as fun at your party and result in fewer arrests and convictions, not to mention lawsuits against the authors. Here are a couple of suggestions:

Shufflefish—Think "shuffleboard" but substitute humorously large rubber fish for the pucks, mops for sticks, and a large moistened plastic tarp for the board. Traditionally played by elderly pirates at Salty Arms Rest Home for Sea Dogs and Wenches Who Wear Purple, the game found resurgence in league play during the late 1980s. Wacky rule: Frozen salmon may be used instead of rubber fish but only in time-limited games.

Captain's Cannonade—This is a game for couples—or two completely unrelated people who don't mind giving or receiving a public spank on the ass to or from a complete stranger. Simply put, the rules call for a competition of noise made by one member of the pair (the Cannon) who is "set off" (spanked) by his or her partner (the Powder Monkey), resulting in his or her making as loud an "Arrrr!" as he or she may be able. The Cannon "assumes the position" and the Powder Monkey (working the crowd as part of his or her preparations) goes through an elaborate improvised ritual to prepare to "set off" the cannon. Upon impact, the Cannon must then sell the audience on his or her power by bellowing a mighty "Arrrr!" The teams compete and the winner is determined by the enthusiasm of the applause of the partygoers not participating. (Authors' note: We know this sounds like a dumb-ass game, but trust us—adults really get into watching another adult get spanked. We don't fully understand this phenomenon—we have just observed it. Perhaps an anthropological study is in order. Is Dr. Jane Goodall available?) Wacky rule: Tiebreakers are determined by the judges based on the amount of force the Powder Monkey uses to "set off" the Cannon.

Galley— The area of the ship where the cooking takes place. Refer to any kitchen as a galley and you'll be right in pirate style. Refer to your spouse as a "galley slave" and you'll be living in pirate style in the doghouse.

Gibbet— A wooden framework or cage from which dead pirates were hung as an example to others. On September 19, any time you're in a position of public display, you could say you're in a gibbet. We suggest you make a speech about the pitfalls of villainous company.

Top Ten Pirate Toasts

10. May your beard wicks stay lit and your powder dry!
9. Here's hopin' yer six-inch guns give a twelve-inch bang!
8. To manly men and the wenches what gives them permission!
7. To Davy Jones and all the wee little Joneses.
6. Here's to me blunderbuss—the number one cause of cavities in Spanish sailors.
5. May your lovers have moxie, be foxy and not a bit poxy!

4. A cutlass will rust, we'll all turn to dust so do what ye must—grab a handful o' bust, give in to yer lust and say, "In *me* I trust!"
3. Blood and water—blood and water! Everyone is cannon fodder!
2. May the hole in which ye buried yer treasure be twice as deep as the hole in which we'll bury ye!
1. We cast our lot. We took a chance. We've sailed from Perth to Calais, France, and hardly ever changed our pants. We'll end up doin' a hempen dance.

The Drinks

While the games are fun and all, people REALLY come to parties for the fellowship of friends and loved ones. This, of course, is made possible only through the shame-stifling, opinion-emboldening, pain-deadening effects of our favorite social lubricant—alcohol. And for a pirate party, all alcohol is welcome and encouraged, assuming all those attending are of the legal drinking age. (Remember, kids, it's for your protection, and has nothing to do with saving the good stuff for us!) Beer, ale, wine, Everclear in a tub of fruit and fruit juice (deadly) and, of course, RUM! But if you are the bartender for the evening, we have a couple of recommendations—some "Dos and Don'ts for Pirate Party Bartenders."

DO—Refer to everyone as "matey," "me hearty" or "me saucy dumplin' o' luv!"

Glory hole— Our very favorite name for the privy. "Privy" is our second favorite name for the privy.

Gunwales, or gunnels— The upper edge or wall of the ship, so called because the guns were mounted on it. Try using it in reference to any high partition, including the side of the booth in a bar or restaurant, or your cubicle at work. Or you could just put up your hand and say, "Talk to the gunnels."

DON'T—Use anyone's real name. They are drinking to forget or be forgotten.

DO—Let partygoers call you "Isaac from *The Love Boat*" and give them the double-finger-point thumbs-up sign.

DON'T—Allow anyone to start singing *The Love Boat* theme. Nobody knows the words but everyone will join in anyway.

DO—Accept tips and drunken declarations of love.

DON'T—Accept tips and drunken declarations of war. (Foreign Service only.)

DO—Serve some drinks in a coconut shell.

DON'T—Serve any drinks in an enemy's skull.

DO—Steer all conversations away from politics.

DON'T—Steer your Pontiac into politicians. (On second thought—DO!)

DO—Offer the children something nonalcoholic and keen.

DON'T—Encourage the children to "lick the shot glasses clean."

QUICK QUIZ

1. Who are the five people, living or dead, you'd like to invite to your party? Things to consider: Dead people smell funny but don't consume nearly as much liquor.
2. The Pirate Guys take a very peremptory tone in the beginning of this chapter. Do you think they got that from watching Martha Stewart,

and do you kinda like it when they get all strict and demanding? Draw a picture of Ol' Chumbucket or Cap'n Slappy as a dominatrix. Use plenty of red crayon.

3. Which do you find more frightening—Cap'n Slappy's blunderbuss, or Martha Stewart's hot glue gun? Things to consider: chest wounds, decoupage.
4. The authors attempt to limit their liability by telling readers not to play the games they describe, especially the deadly hacking and slashing one. Who COULD you sue in the event that you play it anyway and one of your guests loses a limb? Be creative, and do not automatically rule out people in government. (But DO rule out the authors, of course.)
5. What really ARE the words to the theme from *The Love Boat*? Who sang it? Hum the tune. Now try getting it out of your head.

11
Till Death Do You Part

Hallo, Bubbellah!

Mazel tov on your and Brandi McFadden's upcoming nuptials. I get such nakhes from planning weddings—I can't begin to tell you. I know what you're thinking: "Why is Yenta planning the wedding for a couple of nice goyish kids like us?" Aren't you? Go on, admit it! Well, Brandi's parents belong to the same country club as Moishe and Judith Metzenbaum (that's right, sweetie pie, we can be members now!) whose daughter married a shegetz (who was otherwise a perfect mensch) and after Steve and Barbara saw that wedding, they said to Judith Metzenbaum, "We must have the name of your wedding planner!"

So here I am—Shayna Rosenfeldt, your wedding planner extraordinaire!

So, whose cockamamie idea was it to have a pirate wedding? I can only assume it was yours—you must be meshugge. But since you sold Brandi on the idea, far be it from Auntie Shayna to meddle. I won't kvetch about bupkes, darling—it's your funeral.

Here's what I see. I see colors—black and white—very classy, gorgeous in its simplicity. Pirate flags, what are they called?—I get all furblungit—Roger Jollies everywhere! We keep the candles, we lose some of the flowers (she'll carry an orchid bouquet—me she'll never forgive if I don't fight her on this one) and we replace the rest of the floral arrangements with treasure chests filled with colorful beads the guests take as gifts. Are you with me so far, Bubbellah?

We shmuts up the place—make it look more like a pirate ship than the reception hall at the country club—and call it good.

As for you and your groomsmen's outfits, we gotta talk. Her dress is from grandmother—no discussion there. So you can dress like pirates if you want to, but something nice, no shmates—just classy. Like a pirate would dress for his wedding if his mekhutonim were paying for the room—which they are. If you carry swords, leave them

Jack Rackham
Nickname: Calico Jack
Buckle: Unswashed
Favorite weapon: His keen fashion sense
Smartest move: Anne Bonney
During four years as commander of the *Adventure*, Rackham gained a reputation for ferocity that was as unmatched as it was probably undeserved. The best move Rackham made was going to sea with Anne Bonney and Mary Read in his crew. Anne was his wife, and he smuggled her to sea disguised as a man. Mary was also on board in disguise, with her husband. Both Anne and Mary were far the fiercer of their respective duos. When their ship was cornered by the British, Mary and Anne were on deck trying to fight them off while the other pirates, Jack among them, skulked below. At trial Jack was sentenced to death. When Anne was allowed to see Jack the morning of his execution, she told him, "If you'd have fought like a man, you wouldn't be hanging like a dog." Not the words we'd choose to be remembered by.

Haul a jib— Pout. It obviously has a specific nautical meaning, a "jib" being a sail and "haul" being something you do with a sail. But "to haul a jib" has taken on the meaning of pouting or frowning, and we're damned if we know why. We're sure someone will try to tell us, not that we'll listen. We'll just haul a jib that we didn't think of it first.

alone. No futzing with the weapons and for the love of God, no sword fighting before OR after the ceremony. And, just to be on the safe side, no fighting DURING as well. I did a wedding for a Marine once, and he did that honor guard line with the swords above the bride and groom's heads. It was so hot out all of the boys were schvitzing like a sieve in their dark wool coats and the little one fainted as the couple passed through. Fortunately, there was plenty of ice and they were able to reattach her earlobe, but that could have turned out very bad. So leave the swords alone.

As for your vows, I have a friend from the computer, a pirate nebbish, who goes by the name Cap'n Slappy, and he wrote some pirate vows you and Brandi can use. Believe it or not, they've actually been used in real weddings! No kidding! So use 'em or don't. I'd just as soon we went with tuxes and a nice chuppah, but that's me, not you. You're you. Not me. See the vows below.

> ***Groom:*** *I, Mad Dog ________________, take ye, Saucy ________________, as me heart, me soul, me good wench with a stout right hook, the bright dawn of each new day and the soft bed of each day's night. I promise to love ye and honor ye; to make ye laugh when ye're feelin' out of sorts and pretend to listen to ye when ye babble on and on about nothin' in particular. I will protect ye from the elements and the elephants (should we ever encounter them) as it is my understanding that they can be very large and unpredictable. I will love ye through scurvy and through fire, in*

wealth or poverty, whether ye be near or far. And when I speak of treasure, as I am wont to do, everyone within the sound of me voice will know that what I am really speaking about is ye. All of this will I undertake until there are no horizons left to chase and the rum is gone.

Bride: *I, Saucy ________________, take ye, Mad Dog ________________, as me heart, me soul, me salty jack with a crooked smile, the foggy haze of each new day and the lumpy (but familiar) mattress of each day's night. I promise to love ye and honor ye; to make ye laugh so hard the rum comes out yer nose and pretend to listen to ye when ye babble on and on about nothin' in particular. I will protect ye from my wrath and from giraffes, which I understand are very tall and will sometimes step on people because they are not looking where they are stepping. I will love ye through scurvy and through fire, in wealth or poverty, whether ye be near or far. And when I speak of treasure, as I am wont to do, everyone within the sound of me voice will know that I am daydreaming again. All of this will I undertake until there are no horizons left to chase and the rum is gone.*

Yes, it's schmaltzy, but what do you expect from a schlemiel like Slappy?

So, from there we go to the reception. We drink, we nosh, we grab a little tokus on the dance floor, we go home. End of story. What do you think?

This will be the craziest wedding I've planned

yet. But you know, if we pull this off, everyone will be so farklempt, they'll need to change their eye patches.

Sincerely,

Shayna Rosenfeldt

Shayna Rosenfeldt
Wedding Planner Extraordinaire

Haul in the mainsheet— Sailor talk for some nautical thing that pirates and other sailors did involving sails. You're not likely to ever actually do this. But you could use it in other colorful ways, including commenting that a friend's shirttail is out ("Dave, time to haul in the mainsheet"), his fly is open ("Whoa, Dave! Time to haul in the mainsheet!") or it's time to go ("Well, Dave, I guess it's time to haul in the mainsheet"). It also has potential for being used in a sexual way, but we'll leave that up to you.

12

Pirates at School

Mark, who may well have thrown overboard a good career working with kids so that he could do this Pirate Guy thing, was talking to a boy who was constantly being sent out of the classroom for "scamp-like" behavior. He asked the boy, "What do you want to have happen?" The little boy looked at him in all sincerity and said, "I just want it to be recess all day long."

This seemingly innocent comment led Mark to one of those "BOING!" life-changing realizations, a new personal philosophy that

Heave to— Drop (or heave, get it?) anchor and come to a halt. Did you know that stop signs on the high seas all say HEAVE TO? And instead of being octagonal and red, they are gray and sort of crescent-shaped. It's kind of like, "Heave to if you feel like it, but if not, no biggie—there's nobody out here but you anyway—you could even be naked."

is at the core of pirattitude: a philosophy that says, "C'mon, everybody! It's RECESS ALL DAY LONG!"

Kids love pirates. They don't love clowns or purple dinosaurs nearly as much as they love pirates. Pirates are strong and fun. They are also scary in the same way that roller-coasters, Halloween and jumping on the bed are scary—"fun scary." Pirates can do what they want to, when they want to. NOBODY is going to make a pirate do homework or go to bed early on a school night. Not Mom, not Dad, not the principal.

And some teachers love the learning opportunities lurking under the surface of creative chaos. A little anarchy washing over the tedium of daily routine can bring the spark of discovery to any subject. There is a whole world of "teachable moments" in Talk Like a Pirate Day. The possibilities are as boundless as the open sea.

And for all of you school administrators out there, it's a chance to administer the fun out of one more thing that may bring some joy to life. Everybody wins!

You may have to walk single-file from your classroom to the gym, but there's nothing that says you can't swagger a bit while you do it.

In short, the lesson being taught is that part of being human is to have some fun built into our lives.

School/pirate lexicon

School	Pirate ship
Principal	Admiral
Teacher	Cap'n
Teacher's aide	Bos'n
Homework	Scutwork
Gym class	Keelhauling
Classmates	Crew
Spitball	Cannonball
Lunch	Mess
Cafeteria food	Subsistence rations
Metal ruler	Cat-o-Nine-Tails*
Pay attention!	Avast!
School mascot	Ship's goat
School nurse	Sawbones
Bully	Rogue
Good friend	Me bucko
Detention	Davy Jones' locker
Skipping school	Taking shore leave
Leave school at the end of the day	Disembark
Recess	Mutiny
Pop quiz	Surprise attack
Oral test	The Inquisition
Final exam	Executioner's dock
Lunch lady	Gruel wench
PTA	Tribunal of law and order

*Corporal punishment in the classroom has, of course, been severely restricted to schools like the Marquis de Sade's Academy for the Fidgety (home of the Fighting Safe Words!), so this entry is obviously dated. But to adult readers, especially those who had Sister Ann Thomas as their sixth-grade teacher, this will ring a bell. Hell, it may bring back memories that send you to a psychiatrist.

Anne Bonney
Born: A demure young lady in Charles Town
Buckle: Swashed and then some
Libido: Reportedly on overdrive
There is no historical evidence that Anne and her fellow female pirate, Mary Read, were anything other than friends, and tough, roguish pirates to boot—the toughest aboard Jack Rackham's ship. But the whole subject of lesbian pirates has taken an unhealthy hold on Cap'n Slappy's imagination. It's an obsession, almost all he ever thinks about. "You've gotta love the girl-on-girl pirate action," he has been known to say over and over. And over. When Ol' Chumbucket tells him to snap out of it and get back to work cuz there's piratin' to be done, Slappy just gets this dreamy look on his face and stares off into space while the battle or storm or whatever rages on around him. But we're supposed to be talking about Anne Bonney here, and darn, we're almost out of space. She was a pirate.

School	Pirate ship
Staying after school	Taking the dogwatch
Suspension	On leave
Expelled	Marooned
The short bus	The johnnyboat

Hornswoggle— Cheat. Frankly, we weren't aware of this being particularly piratical—sounds more like a word from the Wild West to us—but we found enough references to make its inclusion here plausible, and it certainly has a fine ring to it. And we think Yosemite Sam would make a great pirate.

Things to Do in the Classroom

Teachers, here are a few things you could try in your classroom to use Talk Like a Pirate Day in an educational way.

Hornpipe— Both a single-reeded instrument sailors often had aboard ship, and a spirited dance that sailors do. We don't have a lot to say on the subject, other than to observe that the common term for being filled with lust is "horny," and "hornpipe" then has some comical possibilities. "Is that a hornpipe in your pocket, or are you just glad to see me?"

- Learn your nautical directions. Starboard is right, port is left, stern or aft are back and bow or forward are the front.
- Organize a treasure hunt either in the classroom or on campus. The "treasure" may be little more than an envelope with some classroom currency or a bag of M&M's, but it is the following of directions and clues that makes this a fun and educational activity.
- Visit a maritime museum or view a video on the history of seafaring.
- Have the students invent their own pirate name or their own Jolly Roger. (There is a great deal of information on the Internet about the individualized flags that pirates flew.)
- Pirates elected their captain. Talk about the democratic process and see how it applies to their community, school and classroom.
- Discuss global positioning and how seafarers such as pirates used the same naviga-

tional system that we do today (longitude and latitude). A fascinating episode of PBS' *Nova,* "Lost at Sea: The Search for Longitude," talks about an unlikely hero in solving the problem of finding your way at sea, a guy who invented a reliable clock. It could be a great jumping-off place for this discussion.

- Have the students write and perform their own pirate play. This activity could involve outlining a story, writing dialogue, designing costumes and sets, and developing other theater skills.
- **Most of all have fun.**

TLAPD at School: The Rationale

Cap'n Slappy was once asked,

Me mates an' I be formin' the Pirate Student Union in our hateful prison ship, er, high school, an' we be needin' to justify our existence to the administrators. Fer some reason they demand that we be includin' the community in our raison d'etre. We can only say that we'll talk like Wallace Beery and act like Errol Flynn—only when it be appropriate, o' course. Can ye be helpin' us out in some way, p'rhaps by givin' us some idea to convince the whoresons to approve our Union?

THANKS FROM THE PSU,
CAP'N DANIEL ASARNOW
SEMPER ABSURDA
THE FEW AND THE RANDOM

Jack Ketch— The hangman. To dance with Jack Ketch means the same as to dance the hempen jig. Was there a real Jack Ketch, who was a particularly notorious or busy hangman who gave his name to the trade? We don't know, but it's possible. As a side note, John's mother's maiden name was Lynch, and he likes to imagine there was a hangman in the family tree somewhere. Most of Mark's relatives were hanging from the family tree—an apparent cult suicide.

Here is his response (which first appeared on our Web site, www.talklikeapirate.com, in our "Ask Cap'n Slappy" feature).

Ahoy, Cap'n Daniel!

Ye be a right clever lad, ye! If the governor be wantin' a reason, here be three!

1. It be fun. Talk Like a Pirate Day is an act of creativity itself. It allows the individual to find expression via the conduit of a romanticized archetype of the spirit of adventure and courage. It is, in its very soul, an act of hope and the enemy of despair. It is a healer of wounds. The fun that comes hot on the heels of pirate talk finds voice in the laughter of children—young and old alike—and as a revered mainstay of American periodical literature points out to us monthly from the pages of the publication known as the *Reader's Digest*, laughter, my friends, IS the best medicine.

2. It be educational. Pirate talk requires the speaker to amass not only a knowledge of language skills that facilitate the breaking down and subsequent building up of sentence structure and verb conjugation, but exploration of the pirate's world itself demands a discipline of study that includes but is not limited to: apologetics, art, astronomy, biology, cartography, Dutch, economics, English, French, geometry, geography, global studies, history, Latin, life sciences, literature, logic, medicine, meteorology, music, mythol-

ogy, natural science, physical fitness, physics, psychology, Spanish, theater arts, theology and, of course, zoology.

3. Did I mention it be fun? You could have a parade, with preschool children dressed as pirates. That would be fun as well as funny.

Governor, I beseech ye. Young people today need to learn how to create their OWN fun, not have it spoon-fed to them by the corporate, mind-numbing, creativity-pilfering scalawags who brought us the *Survivor* television program and "Grand Theft Auto 17.5!—Everybody Die Now!" When the young people are begging for a chance to make their fun themselves, we should foster and nourish that. It is the hope of this and future generations.

How was that, lad?

CAP'N SLAPPY

QUICK QUIZ

1. School can be a wonderful, magical place where fostering curiosity and creativity breeds personal investment in one's own education. Discuss why we must never allow this to happen.
2. So many schools are named after politicians and poets. Don't you think it's time to name a school or two after pirates (both real and fictional)? Would you send your child to Ol'

Jolly Roger— The pirate flag, featuring the skull and crossbones over a black field. Many pirate ships had their own distinctive version of this basic flag, so you could tell at a glance if a particular pirate was bearing down on you. And here's another place where we know more than we're comfortable with, but feel a need to pass this knowledge on to you (hoping you might have some idea what to do with it). The words "Jolly Roger" may (we say MAY, because no one knows for sure, certainly not us) come from the French words *joli rouge*, meaning "pretty red," a description of the bloody banner flown by early privateers. This term was corrupted to "Jolly Roger" by English buccaneers and was later applied to the black flag. Who knows? That could even be right.

Chumbucket Middle School? (Home of the Fightin' Fish Guts! Go, Guts!)

3. Pirates are "fun scary." Can you think of anything else that is "fun scary?" Do we need to update the student handbook to keep those things out of school? Draft a proposal.
4. Which is the strongest argument AGAINST celebrating Talk Like a Pirate Day in school?
   a) Pirates were rotten, rotten people who did rotten things and it's not funny because they are just big meanies!
   b) Talking like a pirate celebrates poor grammar and elocution. It's bad enough kids today use the guttural noise "s'up" as a greeting!
   c) It's inviting chaos. Do you want to invite chaos? Why don't you just send chaos a written invitation? What kind of person are you, inviting chaos like that?
   d) Somebody is going to bring a toy sword or a gun or a hook to school and it's going to go from Talk Like a Pirate Day to Arm the Mob and Take over the Office Day and ultimately, somebody's going to put an eye out.
5. If kids are asking Cap'n Slappy for advice, isn't that evidence that education has failed? What shall we spend all that tax money on?

13
TOTLAPPI

So, ye be a pirate. Now what? Do ye even know where to begin? Aye, we didn't think so. Well, what KIND o' pirate might ye be? Ye have no idearrr, do ye? Alright, get out yer quill and ink—it's time to take a wee personality inventory developed exclusively for piratical types such as yerself. It's called:

Keelhaul— Pirates punished people they didn't like by dragging them under the barnacle-encrusted keel. Besides being underwater for a period of time far too long to be comfortable, the recipients were also usually cut up by the sharp-edged barnacles growing on the hull. We've heard two different descriptions of how this was done: either tossing the bound victim off the bow and letting the ship sail over him from bow to stern, or tossing him off one side and hauling him by rope under the hull and back up the other side. We are not in a position to judge which was the actual process, but we don't think we'd care for either one to be done to us or anyone we call shipmate.

The Official Talk Like a Pirate Personality Inventory (TOTLAPPI)

Arrrrr ye the talk of the dock? Cock of the walk? Rank of the plank? Do the mates want to be like ye and the beauties want to be with ye? Well thar, bucko, this little personality test will tell ye and everyone else just what kind of pirate ye be . . . and are meant to be. Thar be two separate tests—one for me mateys and one for me beauties. Ye decide which one ye be. Answer the questions in truth and we'll not scuttle your tub. Lie, and may the sharks have mercy, for Davy Jones knows we won't.

MATEYS

Grub and Grog

1. After a busy day of smiting bull cocks and fancy lads alike with a belaying pin, I can be counted on to wash down the taste of my domination with:
   a) a tankard or two—or six—of ale. And leave me the hell alone!
   b) a nice Barbera D'Alba, from Italy—four or five years old and allowed to breathe for ten minutes before it ever TOUCHES crystal
   c) rum, straight from the bunghole, while

the lads raise the barrel over my reclining manly form

2. Lashing captives to the mizzenmast is hard work and makes any pirate hunger something fierce. The only thing that will quell this buccaneer's belly would have to be:
   a) hardtack—easy on the boll weevils—and salted meat with a tankard of ale—or seven
   b) swordfish in a lime baste garnished with parsley, red potatoes and baby onions
   c) a slab of sperm whale—lightly breaded and herbed and roasted over a hot cannon
3. When I have to be in London for a cousin's hangin' or the pirates' convention, I usually take my meals and drink:
   a) at the Green Dragon, home of the two-quart tankard and slab o' lamb
   b) at the Chateau d' Saucypants. The Prince Regent dines thar weekly and Chef Henri's béarnaise is to die for
   c) in enema form at Mad Sally's Rectal Palace

Fightin'!

4. When locked in fierce combat with an evenly matched foe, my weapon of choice is:
   a) cutlass and dagger, with another dagger clenched in my teeth for added daggerosity
   b) a forty-two-inch foil and another forty-two-inch foil between my teeth for added

Jean Laffite
Nationality: French American
Reputation: Took a hit when he became known as a cartoon character, "Jean LaFoot, the Barefoot Pirate"
The last great pirate operating in American waters, Laffite came to New Orleans from France in 1809 with his brother Pierre, and within a year Jean had become the leader of the pirate colony in Barataria Bay, an island stronghold near New Orleans. During the War of 1812, Lafitte sided with the Americans. He was able to trade his assistance for a pardon, and during the Battle of New Orleans he and his men fought alongside General Andrew Jackson. Laffite moved to Galveston, Texas, and went back into business, playing both sides of the street until driven out by the U.S. government. The two brothers sailed away into legend. While both are said to have continued piracy on the Spanish Main, there is no reliable record of their deaths.

Kelp— Seaweed. There is nothing funny about seaweed unless it is dried, smoked and causes the user to crave Doritos.

Knot— A unit of speed, one nautical mile per hour. A nautical mile is longer than a statute (or land) mile. A nautical mile equals 1.15 miles on land. We assumed the difference had to do with the fact that sailors drink a lot. Turns out there's a perfectly reasonable explanation, which disappointed us so much that we don't have the heart to explain it to you. So let's all pretend that it has something to do with a furious battle involving sea monsters and space people. There, THAT'S exciting!

foilosity, as long as my opponent has a thirty-eight-inch foil. I simply refuse to tussle with a man who has a longer foil than mine

c) pistols, with another pistol dangling seductively from my mouth for added pistolosity. And I would prefer that my opponent be armed with a belaying pin or some fresh fruit

5. I learned to fight:
   a) by punching slabs of meat in the galley until the cook tried to throw me out and I beat him soundly with my fists and forehead
   b) In Paris, under the strict tutelage of the Marquis de Salami, master of the parry and thrust
   c) by throwing smaller men at my opponent. When I ran out of smaller men, I threw vegetables and furniture
6. Fighting is:
   a) an excuse to use me cannon
   b) fabulous aerobic exercise
   c) what we do when we stop using "feeling" words
7. The nastiest scrape I was ever in ended when:
   a) me hook got stuck in a man's skull and I had to lop off his head in order to continue the battle. Well, ye should have seen the terrified looks on the scurvy dogs' faces when they realized I was pummeling them with their own captain's head.
   b) me opponent went to gouge out me eye

and realized he was sticking his thumb through me patch into me empty eye socket! I laughed and shouted, "Too late!" The look on his face was priceless.

c) I stuck my thumb into what I thought was my opponent's eye. Turned out it was just a patch covering his empty eye socket! He laughed and said, "Too late!" But he did it in a way that was just adorable.

Loving

8. The first thing I do when we get into port for wenching is:
   a) grab the sauciest wench in the pub and kiss her like she's never been kissed. Then I drink enough to forget she's had more pirates than baths.
   b) check the latest dispatches from Paris to see what the Dauphin is wearing and where I can find ruffles like those.
   c) size up women. When I find one that is about my size, I drink her under the table, take her up to her room and spend the rest of the night trying on her clothes. Sometimes she drinks ME under the table . . . but I still wake up in her clothes. GOD! I LOVE being a pirate!
9. Those long nights at sea, when I haven't had a woman for months, I find that I:
   a) need to be careful to remember which is the hand and which is the hook
   b) transport myself into ANY French

bordello simply by lighting a few candles, breathing in the salt air and letting the caress of the ocean waves bring me to perfect carnal bliss. Oh, and sometimes I bugger a fancy lad named Kevin

c) I'm sorry . . . what was the question?

Kraaken— A legendary sea monster, usually described as a giant squid with tentacles and suckers and . . . eeeeuw! Featured in one of those "sword and sandal" movies—*Clash of the Titans,* we believe. Immortalized in the line "Release the Kraaken!" Of course, this usage has a sexual connotation we will leave to your warped imaginations.

Treasure

10. To my way of thinking, the perfect treasure would be:
    a) GOLD, fool! More gold than I can imagine! And when I CAN imagine it, I find out that there is MORE gold! Arrrr! It's like I'm CRAPPING gold!
    b) silks from China, china from Italy, French lace and Irish linen—a veritable United Nations of plunder
    c) waking up on the morning of my seventy-second birthday realizing that I have no regrets for the things I have done, only for the things I haven't—and that a life of adventure has been the real treasure

Lassie— A diminutive for "girl," "woman" or "sweetheart." Don't use it in addressing a woman and then make the obvious pun about the famous movie dog. Not if you want to get any that night.

Alright, put down your quills. Remember, like any measurement of personality, this one is biased. It won't predict how far you will go in the insurance business or the medical profession or as an edumacator. It will, however, give any prospective pirate captain an idea if you are (or aren't) a good fit for his crew. Remember, there were no "wrong" answers. Nobody's going to walk the plank or be keelhauled—unless he really wants to.

IMPORTANT NOTE: School psychologists, social workers and clinicians should be wary of using TOTLAPPI when qualifying students for IDEA services, DSM-IV identifications (under ANY axis) or as a part of any professional assessment. Medical professionals are hereby cautioned not to use TOTLAPPI as a tool to determine appropriate medications and/or dosage. Lawyers are hereby notified that the results of TOTLAPPI are not admissible in most state and federal courts with the notable exceptions of the Bahamas, French New Guinea, Madagascar and Wyoming. Amnesty International has requested a moratorium on TOTLAPPI in death penalty cases until the American College of Psychiatry and the British Psychological Association can complete a twelve-year longitudinal study into TOTLAPPI's efficacy rate and cultural bias. This tool was designed for use solely by pirate captains and Web surfers. Please do not attempt this in any professional setting.

If ye answered mostly (a) ye be:

Bloody Tom Bloodroot

Profile: Some men are born great, some achieve greatness and some slit the throats of any man that stands between them and the complete mantle of power. You never met a man you couldn't eviscerate. Not that mindless violence is the only avenue open to you, but why take an avenue when you have complete freeway access? You are the

League— A nautical unit of measurement equivalent to three nautical miles. Just to confuse things further.

Letters of marque— Documents from the government that turned a pirate into a privateer, a ship with government sanction to raid the shipping of other countries. This didn't mean their activities were any more legal in the sense of international law, nor were captured privateers treated more leniently than their unsanctioned brethren. The line between privateer and pirate was a thin one indeed, and many was the privateer who crossed it without realizing it until moments before doing the hempen jig.

definitive man of action. You are James Bond in a blousy shirt and drawstring-fly pants. Your buckle was swashed long ago and you have never been so sure of anything in your life as in your ability to bend everyone to your will. You will call anyone out and cut off his head if he shows any sign of either taking you on or backing down. You cannot be saddled with tedious underlings, but if one of your lieutenants shows an overly developed sense of ambition he may find more suitable accommodations in Davy Jones' locker. That is, of course, IF you notice him. You tend to be self-absorbed . . . a weakness that may keep you from seeing enemies where they are and imagining them where they are not. Romance only clouds your judgment more. Do not, under any circumstances, allow yourself to be "in love." You will lose your edge—and most likely your head.

If ye answered mostly (b) ye be:

Lord Percival Fiddlefaddle

Profile: Some say you are a fop. Some are right. Well, not in that you are a fop (although you may well be and there is nothing wrong with that). You are a very fashion-conscious fellow. However, you are not the dashing swashbuckler you had hoped you would be when you started "this pirate thing," as Mumsy called it. You are very interested in the latest dance craze sweeping the Court. You worry that your sleeves may have too much or too little poof to them. You are also, to the surprise of many, a fierce fighter. Your loyalties shift like the wind, but that's what sails are for. You are not brutal, but you certainly can be cruel. Self-possessed, self-aware and self-absorbed, you make Narcissus green with envy. You're not above "cheating," but to your way of thinking, that's just playing the game better than anyone else. However, if you woke up one day and found yourself captain, you would devote your considerable mind to finding a way OUT of it. You like influencing power . . . not wielding it.

If ye answered mostly (c) ye be:

Devilish Danté Smackbottom

Profile: You, sir, are an activist! You will not only change the world—you will make it dream of you in a Little Bo Peep costume. You are the embodiment of the love that dare not hoist its sail! Ahoy thar! You could make a two-patch pirate turn his head . . . but then he would lose sleep over it and what good would that do anyone? An innovator, you are WAY ahead of your time—and everyone else's. You are sensitive and artsy-fartsy. You say things like "artsy-fartsy," but there is always a slight giggle in your voice when you say it—like Paul Lynde on *Hollywood Squares* delivering a staggering punch line. Speaking of punching, the only punching you would do is "punching up" that outfit with some accessories—

say, a little bandana and some glass beads. You're not the pirate we want in a fight, but we want you there for the crying game that follows! You go, girl.

Line— Ships don't have rope aboard, no matter what you think you see in movies or photos. When it's on a ship it's called a line. Sure, you can call it rope if you want to, but you'll make yourself look like a lubber when you do.

Okay, here's a tricky one—if ye answered all over the board, ye be:

Mad Spikey MacMadder

Profile: You are capable of great sensitivity and creativity. You are also insanely violent and malevolent. Grandmothers will tell frightening stories to children about you—YOUR grandmothers! YOUR children! Just when people think they have you figured out, they become sure that they were wrong, wrong, wrong. Then you prove to them that they were right in the first place only to confuse them three hours later. You are SUCH a tease! Your friends fear your approach. Will you be Mad Spikey or Sweet Spike? Who knows? They never will—and neither will you.

Lubber— A lubber is an incompetent sailor or oaf, or someone who does not go to sea, who stays on the land. The word "lubber" is one of the more fierce weapons in your arsenal of pirate lingo. In a room where everyone is talking like pirates, "lubber" is ALWAYS an insult.

While these stereotypes are broad, they do cover the full range of the pirate experience. Well . . . not exactly the full range. There is another range and it's a thing we like to call "a little something for the ladies."

BEAUTIES

Grub and Grog

1. As a woman, I think about my health when I eat—but I must weigh that against the need to send a clear message to my crew about who I am as a person. When there is talk of a mutiny afoot, my crew can know my mind by reading my menu. At these times, I am inclined to feast on:
   a) the recently slain carcass of a sassmouth bos'n
   b) no carb, high protein. Look, I have GOT to stick with the program, mutiny or no. And then, twenty-five laps around the deck
   c) Oh, do I get to eat now? I haven't had a warm meal in years, what with, "Cap'n, could you get me some ketchup?" And "Cap'n, my chum is cold!" It's a wonder I have found the strength to stay with this ship at all!
2. At the end of a long day of fiery broadsides and plunder frenzies, nothing is quite as nice as a topside nightcap. When the ship's bartender says, "Pick your poison, me beauty," I will inevitably order:
   a) ale . . . well, first, I keelhaul the bartender (what kind of pirate ship has a "bartender"?). Then I drink the ale from his hollowed-out skull until I pass out

Lubber hole— A hole through the platform surrounding the upper part of a ship's mast, through which one may climb to get aloft. We suppose this got the name because a true seaman didn't need the help, but could probably clamber over without the aid, or at least claim to, while a lubber, if he actually made it that high, needed a hole to squeeze through. For the purpose of Talk Like a Pirate Day, the lubber hole would be any tight entry, especially if it helped you get somewhere that might otherwise be difficult, like a shortcut to the men's room in a crowded bar.

b) strawberry daiquiri—definitely a weakness of mine. But I will drink it out of a human skull if that helps. Also (note to self) must schedule an extra midnight flogging to work off the calories. Where does "strawberry daiquiri in a human skull" fit into my caloric exchange program?

c) warm milk and Bailey's Irish Cream . . . oh! I will also treat myself to that Toll House cookie I managed to hide from the first mate. I don't care if it isn't tough—warm milk and Bailey's has a wonderfully soporific effect on me and God knows when I am going to get a full night's sleep

3. You're in port with that special someone and he or she tells you that "tonight is about you." Where do you want to dine and what's on the menu?

a) We are going to the Hook and Bull for hot meat. Then, dinner and drinks.

b) Oh, great timing, Slick. Today is a "liquid protein only" day. You knew that, you bastard! Alright. Let's get this over with.

c) Really? Tonight is about me? Oh, I don't know, where do YOU want to go? We ALWAYS go there . . . but alright.

Fightin'!

4. My philosophy of combat in five words or less is:

a) groin, groin, eye-gouge, groin, head

b) "Eye-gouge" is hyphenated. You can't . . . damn
c) Hang in there—people change

5. The most humorous thing I have ever seen in an all-out fight was that one time when:
a) I lopped off this pirate's head and he took about six or seven steps with his arms waving in front of him as if he wanted to say, "Hey! Where's my head?" To top it off, there was no way he would ever find his head because it had landed in the chum bucket. That still makes me laugh.
b) I was leading the cannonade by running up and down the decks, barking orders and reminding the gunners to thoroughly clean the barrels between volleys, when the realization struck me that I was not only getting valuable aerobic exercise, but also reaping the benefits of the hot, humid, almost saunalike feel of the lower decks. Well, maybe that's not funny to you, but I found it very serendipitous.
c) I was working in the galley one evening when a fight broke out between two pirates. I tried to stop them but they were incensed. I shouted, "Somebody's going to put an eye out!" At that same moment, one of the pirates stuck his thumb through the eye patch of the other pirate who proclaimed, "Too late!" Well, that made us laugh and laugh. Then we had cookies.

Lubber line— A line or mark on the compass that shows the heading of the ship. You could use it in reference to any visual guide that helps you find your way—for instance, using the light post you parked next to as a help in finding your car. For Talk Like a Pirate Day, we think that the global positioning emergency service OnStar should call itself LubberLine.

Madagascar— A large island off the east coast of Africa, a favorite hangout of pirates working in the Indian Ocean raiding the shipping of the Grand Moghul of India and the British East India Company. Also, the last stand of your fragile foothold for African dominance in a game of Risk.

Lovin'

6. If you want to put me in the mood you will need to bring the following:
   a) hemp rope, cat-o'-nine-tails and the ability to leave quickly when I say, "Done. Leave."
   b) a basket of cinnamon-orange potpourri, my pillow from home, six sage candles and some seedless grapes
   c) lots of time, a fresh nightshirt and the ability to talk about your feelings
7. If your sexual exploits were kept in a journal and discovered years later, what would you hope the title of your adventures would be?
   a) *Pride and Extreme Prejudice: Dispatches on Those I Have Dispatched*
   b) *Plunder and Pleasure: A Working Woman's Guide to Self-Actualization on the High Seas*
   c) *Like Salt Water for Chocolate*

Pirate Fashion

8. When selecting an ensemble for the day's busy schedule, I always adhere to the following rule:
   a) enough leather to kill, enough skin to thrill
   b) okay, I don't know who thought the "blue-and-white-vertical-striped pants frayed mid-shin" was a chic look but that is NOT official "capri" attire. And once more, people, spiked bandanas will NEVER make a comeback. Accessories should bring it together, not tear it apart!

c) Dress in layers—you're not the weatherman, are you? And for goodness sake, take a sweater! Sunscreen wouldn't kill you either. Don't give me that look, mister!

9. If your Jolly Roger was ripped from the mast and carried off to sea by an errant cannonball and you had no black cloth with which to make another one, what would you replace it with that reflected your true pirate spirit?
   a) I would execute a prisoner, soak his shirt in his blood, nail his skull and crossed bones to it and fly it.
   b) I've always thought that GREEN was the color of action. Perhaps a green flag with a picture of a cannon on it. It says, "We are ready to take action and we have a cannon!"
   c) Flags are important. They let others know who we are and we can say a pledge of allegiance to them. I have some gingham that I was saving for making tablecloths—we could sew a yellow sun on the gingham, and that way there would ALWAYS be a sun in the sky!

Treasure

10. To my way of thinking the perfect treasure would be:
   a) a golden club hollowed out with chimes in the center that make a pleasing jingle when I smite my enemies hard on the head. Ooooo! With TWO such clubs I could perform a symphony of suffering.

Matey— A shipmate, a friend or buddy. When people live in as close proximity as pirates do, sharing sleeping quarters and pillaging and never doing laundry, mateys can be very close friends indeed.

b) an island, no, wait, TWO islands . . . better yet, a CONTINENT, where I am the absolute ruler and I have thousands and thousands of servants, no, WORSHIPERS, who are both attractive and intelligent and who do my bidding without question. Oh, and they are all mute and crap gold.

c) just one holiday where the entire family was there and somebody says, "Hey, let ME do the dishes this year!"

Me— Replaces "my" in all uses, such as "Come hither, me beauty," or, "Wait'll ye taste me cutlass." Use it to indicate possession. DO NOT use it to replace "I" for the first person singular, as in, "Me was thinkin' of . . ." Save that for Talk Like a Caveman Day.

Thank you, ladies. You may now put down your quills and take a break. Or continue and score your inventory answers to find out just what kind of pirate queen you are . . .

If ye answered mostly (a) ye be:

Mad Molly Hatchett

You have an unspeakably capacious appetite for all things violent. Actually, you are only a heartbeat from running this ship—the captain's heart, which will most likely stop beating while you hold it in your hands. That whole maternal instinct thing was completely left out of your genetic makeup. Intimacy is not your strong suit. Body disposal is your strong suit. You will probably be running the ship before long. You will find, however, that the crew will be more willing to negotiate a peaceful working agreement with the sharks in the open seas than stay aboard Mad Molly's Ship of Indiscriminate Amputations.

If ye answered mostly (b) ye be:

Fabulous Fanny Wigglesworth

I know you are on a very tight schedule so I will keep this brief. You need to loosen up that corset and have an ale . . . or six. Now, I know the ship would get NOWHERE if not for your organizational skills, and without you, the cleaning regimen drops completely off the radar and the next thing you know, we're in the middle of another bilge-rat infestation! But sweet Davy Jones, girl, give it a rest! Your constant struggle is to come to terms with where you ARE and let go of the need to make it where you WANT to be. Besides, Molly enjoys bilge rat . . . and she misses the toasted hardtack ratburgers. Remember, it's "adapt, THEN overcome." You just skip over the adapting part and are engaged in a seemingly endless cycle of overcoming and overcoming. Let it go! We all know you are right—if we sign a piece of paper that says so and can be used carte blanche in any and all circumstances can we please have some cakes with our tea?

If ye answered mostly (c) ye be:

Measure for chains— To be outfitted for the gibbet cage. Since the gibbet cage was largely used to hold dead people or people who were soon to be dead, this was not a good thing to be measured for. You might use it in the sense of being set up: "Looks like I'm being measured for chains," you might say as you notice your co-workers setting you up to take the blame for something. May also have meaning for an S and M club.

Nurturing Nelly Nelson

Now, see? That's what a mommy should look like! I know. I watched a whole lot of TV in the sixties and you are just like June Cleaver and . . . well . . . mostly June Cleaver. Oh, sure, you're a pirate—and I am the starting center for the Minnesota Timberwolves. You may think that all of this is a bunch of silliness, but in thinking that, ask yourself, "Isn't that a 'mommy' way of thinking?" You don't like being treated like a used chum-bucket and you do dream of adventure, but something about the fire in the hearth and dried oatmeal on your child's face brings you back. Now, should a pirate—man or woman—threaten the peace and safety of your family unit, no friendly port would be friendly enough to save them from your tightly pent-up rage. The vengeful carnage that would be unleashed would be of biblical proportions. But tonight, after the quilting bee or the Bunco game you will be checking the children's toothbrushes for wetness and having a little chat with them if they try to pull the old, "yeah, we brushed, smell our breath" thing and their bristles are dry. What happened to you, girl?

If ye answered all over the board ye be:

Motherly Martha Toogood

You are so sweet! You are so sweet we should wrap you in cellophane, lace you with strychnine and razor blades and give you to the children on

Halloween! Now we know where Mad Molly's entire maternal link went. Still, you have a tendency toward violent outbursts that will land you in some shark-infested hot water someday. Your love of children and propensity for ultraviolence should be a good indicator of your readiness to serve as a foster parent for an "at risk" youth. No, you're NOT ready . . . don't even think about it! Also, you have little or no sense of humor. Honestly, you are not funny. Let that whole Roseanne thing go. She wasn't funny, either. If you have children, let them go live with someone who is not related to you. If you are visiting a fertility clinic, stop. Stick to what you are good at—plotting, planning and scraping barnacles.

Thank ye for taking TOTLAPPI. The crack research team and meself hope the insights found here are useful to ye in yer pursuit of the richly rewarding field of international piracy. If ye be not happy with the way TOTLAPPI has summed up yer personality, take it again and give different answers. Someday, perhaps, ye can be the person ye think ye be.

14

Ahoy, Hollywood

In Which the Pirate Guys fantasize about their future in entertainment.

AHOY, HOLLYWOOD!

by Byron "Bunny" Buffington

Hollywood, CA— Yo ho, ho! And hello, sailor! It is I, your favorite pedant of popular piracy, Bunny Buffington, clueing you in on the latest from the wonderful world of Buccaneer Babylon! That's right, me hearties! Swashbucklers have taken Tinseltown by hook AND by crook and are giving it a right good roister as well as a sound saucy swinging. Oooo! Save some for Bunny!

ITEM! It appears that Johnny "Jack Sparrow" Depp isn't the only man in mascara to put on the pirate these days. Rumor has it that the unstoppable Jack "the Human Top" Black and Oscar / Tony / Bunny's Favorite Boy Toy winner Kevin Spacey have been tapped to play Pirate Guy personages "Cap'n Slappy" and "Ol' Chumbucket" respectively in an upcoming movie about their adventures aboard the *Festering Boil*! Quick! Somebody get me a lance and some gauze! The fictional filibusters flashing onto the big screen next summer were developed by none other than those best-selling authors, sexy senior John Baur and his fat, flatulent friend, Mark Summers. The two founders of International Talk Like a Pirate Day had hoped to play the parts themselves, but director Clint Eastwood was unimpressed by their acting resumes, commenting, "Now THAT won't make my day." Apparently one doesn't leap from the stage at Albany (Oregon, no less) Civic Theater and land on screen three at the Applegate Mall's Cineplex 16 or Mission Vallejo's Sunset Six!

A consummate professional, Mr. Spacey has moved in with Baur to study his mannerisms and glean insights into "just what makes a Chumbucket tick." So far, we're told, all he's learned is Mr. Baur's obsessive system for loading the dishwasher. It is rumored that Mr. Black is preparing for his role as everybody's favorite advice-giving, drunken bastard sea captain by surviving for a week in a gorilla pen with nothing but a keg of beer and a willingness to throw his own poo.

Ching Yih Saoa
Nationality: Chinese
Hotness factor: Unknown, but we like to think of her as looking like Lucy Liu
Rating: Best pirate ever

Ching Yih Saoa inherited her husband's fleet of more than six hundred pirate ships that terrorized the South China Sea in the early nineteenth century. The widow flourished as a pirate queen, expanding the fleet to more than eight hundred large junks, thousands of smaller ones, and more than seventy thousand men and women. Nary a ship passed without her approval. She also controlled the coastal cities, demanding massive payments. Any town with the temerity to resist was sacked brutally, and every man, woman and child killed. The Chinese navy tried repeatedly to destroy her, but Ching Yih Saoa maintained her vicious stranglehold on the South China Sea until she eventually accepted a pardon from the frustrated Chinese government and retired to a life of luxury.

Mizzenmast— A secondary mast of the ship. You'd think from the name it might have been set in the middle (mizzen?) of the ship, but you'd be wrong. That's the mainmast. It strikes us that perhaps some speech therapy, or at least orthodontia, might have cleared up communications aboard ship, but our language would be less colorful for it.

When asked what sense any of that made, Summers commented, "Yeah. That's how I did it, too."

ITEM! Reality Series Scuttlebutt—Meanwhile, Disney is negotiating with Bravo TV to create a new "fux [sic] up your life" series based on the popular *Queer Eye for the Straight Guy* premise. They're calling it *Pirate Eye for the Gay Guy*. Every week, a team of six pirates (they're billing themselves as "the Scurvy Six") will attempt to infuse pirattitude into a willing homosexual. (Call me, PLEASE!) The Scurvy Six will move in and just take over! Goodbye candles and matches! Hello cudgels and patches! The Six offer "specialty" skills:

Bloody Bill Fullen will work with contestants on their fighting skills—none of that slappity-slappity stuff with him! We're talking full-contact head butts, people! By the end of the week, our contestant will be bar fighting . . . just like a big brute he-man!

Dapper Danny McCallister is our pirate fashion consultant. But if you think a blousy shirt and tight leather pants are piratty, look out! He builds not just the look, but the smell of pirate haute couture and will leave our contestant looking, if not *fabulous*, certainly *pirate butch*!

Saucy Meg Brown does her best to teach our contestant the art of pirate flirting, but here's the catch—he'll be flirting with *women!* How's that for creepy? She also does arts and crafts.

Blatherin' Bobby Sprague will teach our contestant how to talk like a real pirate. He'll turn that "yoo hoo!" into a "yo ho!" and trade that lateral lisp for a guttural growl. By the end of the week, our contestant's voice will strike fear into the hearts of small children, weasels and invertebrates.

Brick Stanley indoctrinates our brave contestant in the art of all things nautical: what cannons go to port and which go to starboard? Why do they call it a poop deck, and is it okay to giggle when you call it that? And what about those stars? In addition to being twinkly and adorable, what good are they? Brick will let us know!

Sir Ralph Danforth (it's pronounced "Raif" because he is SO ENGLISH) ties it all together in a neat little package with a combination of encouragement and strict discipline! He'll put the final touches on our contestant and if he strokes him just right, he'll look just like all the other seamen—hot and sticky! Oh, Sir Ralph! I know one very lazy Hollywood reporter who would love to meet your cat—the one with nine tails! Mee-owwwwweeee!

After a week of being keelhauled in the pirate lifestyle, the contestant will board an actual pirate ship and test his newfound skills. Will he prove himself to be a *swashbuckler* or a *swishbuckler*? We'll just be glued to our television sets to find out!

ITEM! Brethren o' the Host — It appears that Bob Barker's days are numbered on *The Price is Right*! My insider source says that producers are negotiating with Edward "Blackbeard" Teach (or Blackbeard impersonator Rick Poulette) to take over the hosting duties on the perennially popular game show.

Twenty-three-year-old producer Max Clayton

Moses' Law— Forty lashes with the cat-o'-nine-tails, minus one, which works out to thirty-nine lashes. That's the same number of lashes Pilate ordered for Christ, so to give a man more than that would be un-Christian, although it's hard to imagine pirates caring too much about that. The fact is, thirty-nine lashes are plenty, easily enough to kill. Typically fewer lashes were ordered or administered except for the most serious offenses. The trick seems to have been to make the recipient pass out with pain as quickly as possible to spare him a probable death.

told this reporter, "It's not like Bob's ever going to change—I mean, jeez, he's great and all, a living legend and the most important blah blah blah. We're just going in a new and cooler direction. Also, Bob's got that funky 'old man' smell. That's just gotta go."

When asked what changes in format viewers could expect, Clayton remarked, "Well, for one thing, we'll be gauging the prices in doubloons instead of dollars—and the sexual harassment of the models will occur onstage rather than backstage. It's what our audience wants to see! We're just responding to the shifting demographic." He added, "But we're pretty sure that Blackbeard will also encourage pet owners to spay and neuter their pets—so that's all good, right?"

ITEM! One buccaneer bozo — Not all is grog and booty for pirates and their progeny, we must admit. Dashing dandy Dalrymple Bonnet, the great-great-great-grandson of legendary pirate loser Stede Bonnet, has created quite a reputation as an incontinent whiner after his brief appearance on *The Apprentice*. No one in the video village who watched his performance in the boardroom will soon forget his servile cringing as the Donald began berating him for his team's failure in the first task of the new season. Before the toupeed one could even utter his trademark phrase, Bonnet was on the carpet, literally licking the sumptuous black leather of DT's exquisite Bruno Maglis.

As Herr Trumpenstein started to say the two words all Americans love to hear, "You're fired," the camera clearly caught the growing stain on the inseam of Bonnet's trousers. Here's guessing that the Donald will have to have the boardroom carpet steam-cleaned before next week's episode. And I'm guessing it will be a while before Dalrymple ventures out into the job market again. Well, that's what trust funds are for, eh, Daly?

Still, Bonnet's stain on the boardroom carpet is the only one on the reputation of freebooters in filmdom, as pirates continue to capture the fancy of the public and storm the citadels of power in the entertainment world.

So that's all for now, movie lovers. With a "Yo ho ho" the Bunny will be hopping off until next week. Keep your powder dry. Arrrr!

15
Music Hath Charms

Bet you thought this chapter would be a simple list of sea chanties and concertina classics, right? Wrong. We win the bet and your first-born male child, although Neptune knows the last thing we need is more kids.

Don't get us wrong. The more we get into the whole pirate thing, the more we have been exposed to the form, and there are several sea shanties we actually enjoy singing (and dozens we can't stand, but that's our problem, not yours). But personal musical tastes are personal. Whatever your tastes, your music gives you that internal sound track for your adventuresome lifestyle.

If you're as full of pirattitude as we know you are, then you probably enjoy a rich fantasy life. When you're driving to work, taking a morning walk, sitting at your desk or washing the dishes, there's a good chance that in your mind you see yourself striding a heaving quarterdeck, or standing amidships at the railing, peering at the galleon you're bearing down on, cannons charged. What we want to consider here is, what song is playing in the background of this scenario? If you're like us, it could be anything from the Stones' "Sympathy for the Devil" to Wagner's "Ride of the Valkyries." It wouldn't be anything by the Eagles, because no matter how much we like the band, it just doesn't fit.

We do not recommend a specific musical style or genre. Some people enjoy country-western music. We can't imagine why; we'd rather have our teeth drilled than listen to country-western. But there's no arguing about taste. Those people would probably be equally appalled by our selections. Even between ourselves our musical tastes vary, so that when we have to travel together there is usually a titanic fight over control of the radio. We have been known to come to blows.

Whatever fantasy fills your sails, we encourage you to incorporate the music that appeals to you in every phase of your life. Music should blow you from port to port like a brisk wind in your sails, not just tousle your hair like a priest does to an altar boy.

For example, you don't want to be like Stede Bonnet, the worst pirate ever, constantly singing "Oops! . . . I Did It Again."

Here are a few examples of pop and rock songs and what piratical situations they would best apply to.

Piratical circumstance	Pop song
Sacking a city	"Burning Down the House"
Marooned	"I Think We're Alone Now"
Launching an attack	"Fire"
Blackbeard's ship is heading your way	"Madman Across the Water"
You're sinking (obviously)	"Going Down"
Shore leave	"Margaritaville"
The British Navy is approaching	"Born to Run"
Being marched to the gallows	"Stairway to Heaven"
Counting your booty	"Money!"
Again, counting your booty	"Just Can't Get Enough"
Undergoing a cannonade	"Whole Lotta Shakin' Going On" AND "You Shook Me All Night Long"
A spark found the powder magazine	"Great Balls of Fire"
Shore leave (again)	"When a Man Loves a Woman"
Shore leave yet again OR What the cabin boy doesn't want to hear	"Gimme Some Lovin'"

On the account— Someone who is "on the account" has turned to the piratical life. And he's paying 4.9 percent interest on his credit card.

Piece of eight— A large, silver Spanish coin. It was worth eight reales. Some were actually perforated into eight pie-shaped wedges, and could be broken into "bits," which could be spent individually. Two of these pieces made up one-fourth, or one quarter, of the coin. This is why we sometimes refer to a quarter today as "two bits" (as in the old cheer "Two bits, four bits, six bits, a dollar . . ."). For the record, we're pretty sure this one is true. We saw it in *National Geographic* magazine when we were kids, while looking for the educational photos on "Women of the South Seas."

Chanties or Shanties?

The dictionary accepts both spellings—"sea chanty" and "sea shanty." Either is correct. John prefers "chanty," because the song is sort of a rhythmic chant. Mark prefers "shanty," because he just thinks "chanty" sounds stupid, and he's evil incarnate, and John is editing this section so he gets to say that.

We battled over it for quite a while until we just decided, "To hell with it, both are right so we'll use both interchangeably." We point this out simply so you'll understand that when we shift back and forth between the two spellings, it's intentional. It's not the fault of the editors, who are much too smart for that. It's our fault, because we're both pigheaded.

Music can be the driving force behind sales of automobiles and beer, and these are things that the modern-day Pirate Guy loves. Who doesn't quietly hum to himself "Like a Rock" when he sees a Ford pickup truck? We all do, even though it was Chevy, not Ford, which used the Bob Seger song in its truck advertising. Show us a man who doesn't know that the proper response to "For all you do" is "This Bud's for you!" and we'll show you an accountant.

Music works its way into the psyche of the Pirate Guy in the same way that weevils work their way into the hardtack. It becomes a parasitic infestation on the memory of things and will never let

Sing Along—or Not

Karaoke is a dangerous combination that mixes beer and a LIVE MICROPHONE! Pirate Guys spend a fair amount of time with their pals and mates in bars and taverns, where they often have karaoke night. Guys sitting around drinking, even guys who in their workaday world are doctors or auto mechanics or people in other nonmusical professions, will, under the influence of enough ale, suddenly decide they have the voice of Sinatra—or, even more frightening, Mick Jagger! And, as the police officers are fond of saying when they pull you over, when you drink, the first thing you lose is your judgment.

Musically, Pirate Guys need to be very careful. If you do find yourself in a bar where they're holding karaoke night, make sure you position yourself in the farthest recesses of the booth or table in the back, a spot where you'll have trouble getting out if you try to drunkenly reel to the mike to favor the crowd with your powerful rendition of "I Am Woman." Tell the designated driver in your group that under no circumstances is he or she to let you sing.

Everyone will be happier.

go until your head has been lopped off and sold in a Bombay market to German tourists.

The Modern-Day Sea Chanty—or Shanty

A sea chanty is a work song artificially elevated to the status of classical folk music. The lyrics are almost incidental. It is the rhythm of the song that is important, getting all hands working in unison, such as with the repeated refrain, "Heave away! Haul away!" in the shanty "South Australia."

So if we were looking for a modern-day equivalent, where should we search? Think about it—rhythm is everything, tune and lyrics secondary. Of course, it could only be one thing.

Rap music.

Mark in particular has become a huge fan of the style. His pirate persona, Cap'n Slappy, might almost be referred to instead as Rapmaster Slappy, except that John would probably bludgeon him. He likes to point out that "Cap'n Slappy kicks it OLD SCHOOL." None of his friends know exactly what he means by this, but he does. That's how we came up with "The Drunken Slappy Rap," an unholy marriage between rap and sea shanties. We have performed it several times for live, often drunken audiences, and they seemed to enjoy it. At least, we lived to tell the tale, which must mean

Editor's Note: The craziest thing happened! The Pi-Q scoring guide which was supposed to go on this page got lost while we were putting all of this stuff together. Then our dog, Fluffy, ate it and we got arrested for verbally abusing our dog. Can you believe that? Us?! Arrested?! Anywho, you'll find the revamped and much more complete scoring guide on the back page of this book.

Earworms: The Songs That Never End

This is not a strictly piratical issue, but since this whole chapter deals with adding a sound track to your life to enhance your pirattitude, it seems that, in all fairness, we should add this caveat: The more music you have in your life, the more susceptible you are to the trauma of "earworms."

You wake up in the morning with a song stuck in your head, anything from "A Pirate's Life for Me" to "Stayin' Alive" (always good advice for a pirate), and you just can't shake it. During the course of the day your brain natters on in a torturous replay loop. That's an earworm.

Often it's a song that you know only a few of the words to, so that you repeat just one little part over and over. Not long ago John awoke to find jammed in his brain a small piece of the theme song of *The Real McCoys*, a late 1950s TV series starring Walter Brennan. All day long his brain kept repeating, "With Granpappy Amos and the girls and the boys and the family known as the Real McCoys" with its jaunty "Turkey in the Straw" lilt. Just the process of typing that much has started it again. Aaagghh! STOP!!! NOOO-oo-oo!!! Can't . . . go . . . on . . .

Earworms are hard to combat, almost impossible. All you can do is ignore them and hope they go away, but consciously ignoring your brain is like trying to consciously monitor your breathing. You can try forcing yourself to start thinking of a different, more obnoxious song to cancel out the first, but usually all that does is supplant the old problem, not eliminate it.

The absolute worst earworm of all time is a song that can

strike the brain of anyone, young or old, at any time. It's a song you don't hear often, but which is so sneaky, so omnipresent, that it takes no more than hearing a child hum it to get it firmly lodged in your skull. It's so powerful that we must issue this

WARNING!!

Potential Earworm Coming!

If you do not wish to catch this earworm, we advise you to turn the page NOW!!!!

We refer, of course, to Disney's "It's A Small World."

Sorry. That's all we can write on this subject for now. We have to go lie down and listen to the puppets sing for the next few hours.

something. And they often buy us beer afterward. We take that as a good sign.

We start by getting the audience chanting—"Yo yo yo HO-o, yo yo YO HO." Then Mark keeps 'em chanting while John sings the opening verse or two of "What Do You Do with a Drunken Sailor." Then Mark takes over. Here is the rap part of the song.

The Drunken Slappy Rap

I'm a pirate—a pirate I be
and just like Johnny Depp, it is a pirate's life for me.

Pirate Rounds, The— The route from the Spanish Main to the Indian Ocean. On September 19, it might well be the round of bars you stop at to celebrate and the subsequent circuitous route your room takes when your bed spins.

I sail upon the oceans and I take the seven seas
and I battle false authority and bring it to its knees!
Yo Yo Yo HOOOOOOooooooo!
Yo Yo YO HO!
(. . . with me blunderbuss!)
Yo Yo Yo HOOOOOOooooooo!
Yo Yo YO HO!
He's Chumbucket and I'm Cap'n Slappy.
We gots to make it funky if we wants to make you happy.
We get your toes tappin'—tip tip tappy tappy!
And remember to wear lip balm or your lips will get all chappy.
Yo Yo Yo HOOOOOOooooooo!
Yo Yo YO HO!
(They get chappy now!)
Yo Yo Yo HOOOOOOooooooo!
Yo Yo YO HO!
I kick it with my crew, yeah, we kick it at our leisure.
We're lookin' for adventure but we really want some treasure.
And if we swash our buckle—yeah we're doin' it for pleasure.
We talk like William Shakespeare and his play Measure for Measure
Yo Yo Yo HOOOOOoooooo!
Yo Yo YO HO!
(With the "Thees" and the "Thous"!)
Yo Yo Yo HOOOOOoooooo!
Yo Yo YO HO!

Some people think we're nasty and we're horrible and horrid,
Fightin' battles on the beaches, and we always leave the shore red
With the blood of nameless rabble, and we're takin' what they store-ed
While we pummel all resistance with our savage fists and forehead!
Yo Yo Yo HOOOOoooo!
Yo Yo YO HO!
(With me fists and forehead!)
Yo Yo Yo HOOOOoooo!
Yo Yo YO HO!
(Shake your booty!)
Yo Yo Yo HOOOOoooo!
Yo Yo YO HO!
(Avast!)
Yo Yo Yo HOOOOoooo!
Yo Yo Yo HO!
Fifteen men on a dead man's chest—Yo ho ho and a bottle of rum!
Fifteen men on a dead man's chest—Yo ho ho and a bottle of rum!
Fifteen men on a dead man's chest—Yo ho ho and a bottle of rum!
Fifteen men on a dead man's chest—Yo ho ho and a bottle of rum!
Fifteen men on a dead man's chest—Yo ho ho and a bottle of rum!

Plank— That thing from which pirates were reputed to make captives walk, hands bound, into the drink. The fact that there is little or no evidence that they actually did this is immaterial. Thanks to literally hundreds of movies and books, it is firmly embedded in pirate lore and nothing can be done—either by a couple of louts like ourselves or by prissy, purse-lipped academics—to ever change that. There is some suggestion that the first pirates to actually make someone walk the plank got the idea from reading a book about pirates.

QUICK QUIZ—QUESTIONS FOR DISCUSSION

1. Compare and contrast: "sea chanties" or "sea shanties." Which do you prefer and why? Be prepared to back up your answer with violence, if necessary.
2. True or false.
3. What were the five worst earworms you've ever had? List them in order of severity. Now try to get through the rest of your day.
4. In "The Drunken Slappy Rap," why does Mark (Cap'n Slappy) bring up lip balm? Is it a metaphor, or was he simply too drunk to think of a better rhyme?
5. Why does John (Ol' Chumbucket) refuse to take part in karaoke? Does he think he's too good, or is he a party pooper, or what? Discuss.

16
Gazing into the Future

In Which the apprentice pirate learns how to study the stars and other signs for a clue to the future, and other useless knowledge.

Plunder— Another word for "booty" or "treasure." Also, as a verb, to loot, raid or otherwise attack a prize and make off with the goods on board. It can also be a noun describing what was taken. So you can plunder the plunder, but that sounds a little redundant, so we prefer plunder the loot or loot the plunder.

Poop— The poop is the superstructure at the stern of the ship, typically where you'd see the captain standing, looking dramatic.

For the average pirate, gazing into the future probably wasn't much of a preoccupation. It wasn't hard to guess the fate of most pirates—an uncomfortable end either in battle, at the end of a rope, by drowning or by starving on some godforsaken spit of land on which you'd been marooned.

And anyone caught lounging about the water cask, opining about the stars and their cosmic destiny and practicing the line, "Hey, babe! What's yer sign?" was likely to get a reading from the quartermaster, who'd say something like, "I'll tell ye yer future. I see ye gettin' about thirty lashes from the cat if ye're not back up the rigging in three seconds. ONE . . ."

Still, pirates were not completely immune to the lure of the mystic realm, and from time to time adapted land-based systems in their attempt to divine the future. Here are two of the most popular, as we like to imagine they might have been.

The Signs of the Piradiac (Pirate Zodiac)

Aye, pirates saw the same stars as everyone else—they just saw them a wee bit differently. Where landlocked astrologers might have seen a set of scales or a fish, pirates have seen somewhat darker, more violent signs. They are, as follows:

Cannon (August 22–September 21) A fiery one ye be! Goin' off at the drop o' a head is yer specialty. Ruthless and powerful, yet immovable and cold. All the other pirates talk nice-as-ye-please about ye to yer face. Nobody will tell ye what they REALLY think.

If ye weren't a pirate, ye might be a corporate executive, a police officer or a physical education teacher.

Predicted outcome: Ye'll hang for sure.

Belayin' Pin (September 22–October 19) Ye just want to get the job done! "Dammit, why's this job takin' so long?" ye say. See? I told ye that ye wanted to get the job done. Ye don't really listen to anyone else. But ye're versatile. "Multitaskin'" is what the kids call it these days.

If ye weren't a pirate, ye might be an office manager, a police officer or a wedding planner.

Predicted outcome: Ye have a date with the gallows.

Bone Saw (October 20–November 18) Aye, ye be a curious wee scamp! Ye wonder "How's this thing work?" and "Who's that fellar thar in that British officer's uniform?" A good planner, ye'll organize many a pillagin' party and ye won't leave it until ye've taken every last doily from every last granny in town!

If ye weren't a pirate, ye might be a research scientist, a doctor or the owner of a lawn mower engine repair shop.

Predicted outcome: Picture this—a yardarm and a rope.

Barbarossa
Field of operations: The Mediterranean
Advantage: Tag team
Beard: Pointy, and red, of course
The terror of the Mediterranean, Barbarossa was actually two men—Greek-born Turkish brothers who terrorized the coasts of Spain, Italy and Greece during the sixteenth century. The first, the elder brother Arouj, eventually became ruler of Algiers, but his behavior as a head of state was not notably more temperate than it had been as a pirate, and his subjects appealed for help from the king of Spain. Arouj died in battle with the Spanish in 1518. His younger brother, Khidr, took over the family business and made a better job if it. Swearing allegiance to the sultan of Turkey, he was given the post of governor general of Algiers. From that vantage point he became the undisputed ruler of the Barbary Coast.

Prow— The nose or front of the ship. Its use when describing a well-endowed woman is obvious.

Quarter— Mercy. And rare was the pirate who took or gave quarter. In sitting around talking smack with your pirate buddies, give no quarter. Incidentally, there is a magazine called *No Quarter Given* written for pirate aficionados. Ironically, *No Quarter Given* magazine comes out quarterly. Go figure.

Blunderbuss (November 19–December 21) Aren't ye the sensitive one? Oh, sure, ye can be explosive and are easily manipulated to "go off," but after a long day o' killin' and pillagin' all ye really wants is to curl up with yer journal and write about yer feelin's. It looks as if SOMEBODY needs a hug.

If ye weren't a pirate, ye might be an actor, a psychologist or a colorful street performer.

Predicted outcome: Ye'll avoid "Jack Ketch" altogether by taking a cannonball directly to yer face.

Cutlass (December 22–January 19) Ye're sharp and decisive! Ye're also scrupulously truthful, but willing to work on that. Ye show great initiative and leadership under fire while still enjoying long walks on the beach and those fancy drinks served up in a coconut shell with a tiny paper umbrella. Ye likes what ye likes!

If ye weren't a pirate, ye might be a firefighter, a military officer or a livestock auctioneer.

Predicted outcome: Aye, ye'll hang. But ye'll know ye had it comin'.

Brace o' Pistols (January 20–February 22) Perfection. That's all ye expect from everyone and everything around ye! Perfection. "Is that too much to ask?" ye say. Ye look to the details and ye see even smaller details which seem to be out of sorts—but then ye notice that the even smaller details have wee, tiny details which are clearly chaotic. Ye're a lot o' work.

If ye weren't a pirate, ye might be an engineer, an air traffic controller or a Romanian gymnast.

Predicted outcome: The last thing ye'll say is, "Ye did that knot all wrong!"

Harpoon (February 23–March 21) Ye seek balance in the world. A day is not complete unless ye have both ruthlessly pillaged a town AND raised money for a covered playground for the children. Will nobody think o' the children?!? Well, ye will. Half the time, at least.

If ye weren't a pirate, ye might be a social worker, a judge or a high-wire circus performer.

Predicted outcome: Ye'll be hanged and yer eyes will be donated to a little blind girl named Martha.

Dagger (March 22–April 20) And a poisonous dagger it be, too! Ye're a sneaky one, ye are! And that's just fine for a pirate. Yer stealth comes naturally, but ye also work very hard to see that ye improve yer skills. Ye're natural in the art o' deception—the whole truth thing seems like naught but an intellectual construct for weaker minds.

If ye weren't a pirate, ye might be a spy, a computer software salesperson or a Catholic priest.

Predicted outcome: Ye'll fall to yer death from the prison wall during an escape attempt on the night before ye were due to hang.

Cat-o'-Nine-Tails (April 21–May 25) Ye're the adventuresome sort! Always on the prowl for that new life experience—that rush o' the unknown. Too many days at sea and ye'll be itchin' for somethin', and it won't just be the lice. When thar be a landin' party, ye're the first to volunteer, not having learned anything from watching all those *Star Trek* episodes where the ensign on the away team ALWAYS gets killed before the first commercial. If ye haven't done it yet, ye will. And if ye didn't like it, it wasn't worth doin'. But ye're glad ye did.

Quarterdeck— The stern portion of the upper deck of the ship. Not to be confused with *Quarterduck*, an animated feature in which Donald Duck leads his team to the Superbowl only to discover that he has liver cancer. The movie ends with him being served as foie gras.

If ye weren't a pirate, ye might be a mountain climber, a test pilot or a twentieth-century existential novelist.

Predicted outcome: Ye'll be the giddiest pirate swingin' from the yardarm and wonderin' to yerself, "What comes next?!"

Room to swing a cat— While this seems like an odd way to measure a room, it's actually a practical matter. Of course, it has nothing to do with Kitty. The cat (cat-o'-nine-tails) was the whip used to punish miscreant sailors, and those floggings took place out on deck, because belowdecks there wasn't room to swing a cat. It would be a mighty impressive room on a mighty impressive ship that had that much space.

Iron Bar (May 26–May 28) Ye're austere and cold-blooded. Ye don't NEED much but ye DEMAND everythin'—from yerself as well as everyone around ye. But ye're strong. Sweet Poseidon's pitchfork, ye're strong! And ye're good with words. Ye only use a few to get yer point across—the rest o' the explanation comes with a beatin'.

If ye weren't a pirate, ye might be a mortician, a school administrator or an Amish farmer.

Predicted outcome: Self-disembowelment and hangin' yerself from yer own intestines so as not to waste perfectly good hemp.

Barbed Fishnet (May 29–June 30) A free spirit, ye be. Not one to be possessed or controlled by anyone else, ye go where ye want to go and do what ye want to do. Ye seek to be connected to all things. But all too often, "all things" file a restrainin' order against ye—AND FOR NO

GOOD REASON! But that's alright, ye'll just do somethin' artistic and heal yer wounded soul.

If ye weren't a pirate, ye might be a singer/songwriter/dancer, an independent bookstore owner or a community college macramé instructor.

Predicted outcome: Burnin' to death when ye try to set yer noose on fire to see "if that hemp has any leftover BUD residue in it."

Hook (July 1–August 21) Sharp-witted and ethereal, ye have a dreamy quality about ye. When things go poorly, ye'll find the silver linin' and when they go well, ye'll tell everyone, "See? I told ye it would work out fine." Ye can make meanin' out o' any event—in fact, yer wisdom will be looked to by yer peers and could be very marketable in the publishin' industry.

If ye weren't a pirate, ye might be a political analyst, a game show host or a Nintendo game consultant.

Predicted outcome: Of course ye'll do the hempen jig, but before the trapdoor opens, ye'll notice a man in the crowd with no shoes. As ye fall, ye'll kick yer boots in his direction. Somebody wins.

The Years of ARRRRR Lives

Aye, the years they come, and the years they go—and nobody can tell us different! And just as the Chinese had a system whereby twelve animals represented the nature of a person born during that animal's rotation, so, too, pirates had a belief

Salt, or salty— A salt is someone who is wise to the ways of the sea. The sea is, of course, salt water, so a person long exposed to it is . . . salty. Salty language tends to be coarse, but hey, so is unrefined salt.

Scut— A small crack or chink in the deck.

that there were animal characteristics that could be applied to a person born in a given year.

But the pirates' "Animal of the Year" calendar is much less complicated—instead of twelve there are only ten, mostly because we just couldn't think of twelve. These are, of course, animals with which the pirate would easily identify. There's an old pirate saying that goes, "When ye're a squid, ye're a squid all the way, from yer first salmagundi to yer very last day!" (We go on in that vein for a while—it's quite tuneful.)

All you need to know to identify your place in the Pirate Animal Calendar is the last number in the year of your birth.

1—The Year of the Manatee

"Living large" is your watchword—actually, your TWO watchwords—perhaps not so much two "watchwords" as two "themes"—check that, make it singular. Let's try this again. You live large. Also, you are indecisive—which is strange because you are so smart—deceptively smart. That's it! You have managed to lower others' expectations of you to the point that you don't have to do much to be impressive. And that's fine. You don't WANT to do much. You just want to "Live large." (Whatever that means.)

2—The Year of the Tuna

You are useful and underappreciated. A giver by nature, you do and do and do for others with little or no thought to your own well-being. But secretly, you plot and wait. There will come a day when you will rise up and make the ingrates pay for their ingratitude! Oh, yes. There will be blood on the decks! Bide your time, little tuna. And, if you don't mind, could we mix up your meat with mayo and sweet relish, put you between two slices of white bread and send you off to school in the kids' lunch box? Thanks.

3—The Year of the Pufferfish

Our old shipmate Cementhands McCormack once referred to the pufferfish as "the piano movers of the sea." He was blistering drunk at the time, so we don't really know what he meant by that. But people born under this sign tend to be sensitive and creative. They have the ability to look more intimidating than they actually are—it's called "acting," you should try it, Keanu Reeves. But in the dire moment of being swallowed whole by a predator, the mighty pufferfish can inflate his body in the mouth of the aggressor, killing both predator and prey, which is small consolation, we agree, but still, it's something. Perhaps this is what has led to the popular bumper sticker DON'T FUCK WITH THE PUFFERFISH.

4—The Year of the Monkey

Monkeys are funny and lighthearted. Don't expect a monkey to sit still during a lecture on photosynthesis. They can't—they're monkeys, for gawd's

Scut work —Any tedious, usually maddeningly detailed, work, like scraping the hull or polishing the brass. Today that could run the gamut from doing the inventory at a hardware store to almost any household task you could name—dishes, laundry, cleaning the grout, you get the idea.

sake! Monkeys are also smart, but it is a practical intelligence. They're not going to be flashy or pretentious, unless it gets a laugh. While brevity may be the soul of wit, the monkey knows that "well-flung shit is the height of comedy." And don't forget that monkeys have contributed greatly to many fields, including science, music (when accompanied by a stereotypical Italian organ grinder) and apparently, if you get enough of them at an infinite number of typewriters, literature.

5—The Year of the Squid

Scurvy— This is a shipboard disease caused by improper nutrition. The word goes particularly well with "dog." "Ye scurvy dog, ye!" (Technically, it is caused by a diet deficient in vitamin C, and is characterized by spongy, bleeding gums, bleeding under the skin, and weakness. If that helps at all in your use of the term.) Treatment? Eat a lime.

Oh, you squiddy, you! You're a planner, you are! Organized and flexible, you have contingencies coming out the ass! Literally! If you are being pursued and have to run for your life, you can change directions instantly and spray some "ink" as cover while balancing your checkbook at the same time. Multitasking is your middle name—well, perhaps not your REAL middle name, but if you felt like it, you could easily organize the paperwork to change it. You're slippery and if trapped on an unfriendly deck of an unfriendly ship, it would take little effort to slip under the gunnels and make your escape to sea.

6—The Year of the Parrot

Did somebody order some sass? That's you! Beautiful and self-possessed, you are ever the artiste. To your way of thinking, you are simply holding up a mirror to nature—so long as that "nature" is you. Creativity is overrated—you take others' creativity and make it your own. Why should YOU do all the hard work? Still, you know how to charm and that will carry you far—on somebody's shoulder. Oh, and don't worry about your mess. Somebody with thumbs will clean that up for you.

7—The Year of the Ship's Goat

In a world populated by victims, you are their Royal Highness. Fortunately, the mysteries of life—"Why are we here?" "Is there a God?" "Who let the dogs out?"—hold no power over you. Your strength is in your ability not to care. This lack of curiosity might be a detriment to others, but it serves you well. And in reality, you may be on the receiving end of much abuse without ever being aware that it WAS abuse—so, perhaps, maybe it wasn't. But you never get that far in the intellectual process. Your most aware moment comes when you can articulate an event—ANY event—with a "Huh?" But don't change a hair for us—not if you care for us.

8—The Year of the Shark

You are the picture of focused, ruthless power. Leave the moralizing and hand-wringing to those with morals—and hands. A natural-born leader, you hold both your followers and your victims in equal contempt—but you know how to make use of them all. You prefer the straightforward aggressive approach, but if there is a more expedient

Sea dog—A seasoned, hard-core sailor, one who has looked on storm and gale and braved the worst the sea can offer. Francis Drake was a sea dog. His dog, Scraps, was a sea dog's sea dog.

Sea legs—Sailors, by definition, spend a lot of time at sea. They are conditioned to unconsciously adjust themselves to the rising and falling of the boat in heavy weather. This ability is described as "having good sea legs." It's always amusing to watch people with good sea legs just after they disembark. Often they keep adjusting to the rising and falling, even when they're on dry land.

way, you are willing to look at it. Then you will go ahead and do exactly what you want to do. When someone challenges your worldview, you show your openness by waiting until they are finished before you kill and eat them. But you also have no equal in letting down your hair, or dorsal fin, or whatever it might be that you would let down. You welcome a social event. You haven't been to a feeding frenzy yet that you didn't enjoy. Rock on, shark dude!

9—The Year of the Barnacle

You are bone solid and deeply attached to the world you know. Some go in search of adventure—you wait until it comes to you. Largely ignored by the world around you, you just seem to blend into the crowd and when something bad happens—somebody cuts a leg or something—it will be impossible to pin it on you. You don't share much of your feelings, but you like crowds and want to be where the action is, so long as IT comes to YOU. But resist the temptation to stay attached to moving objects—you'll just end up being scraped away.

0—The Year of the Remora (you know, those little sucker fish that attach themselves to sharks)

More than most, you enjoy hanging around power and getting the visceral rush of all the violence and action, but you don't want to get involved. No, sir. You're happy enough just attaching yourself to the nearest shark and going for a ride, watching the scenes of carnage unfold without taking part yourself. There will be some juicy scraps for you later, but you'd rather not have to do anything to earn them other than hanging on. If it sounds like we disapprove, remember that there're plenty of honored examples of this behavior in the real world—member of a rap star's posse or a boxer's entourage or deputy aide to the assistant deputy press secretary at the White House, to name just a few.

QUICK QUIZ

1. Using your Piradiac Sign and your Pirate Birth Year Symbol, calculate what day you will die. Compare with your friends and relatives to determine, once and for all, which of you is the biggest loser.
2. Which of the following choices most closely reflects your own feeling about astrology?
   a) Astrology is an absurd superstition developed by people who didn't know WHAT stars are, let alone where they are.
   b) I never leave the house in the morning without consulting the newspaper astrology column.
   c) Stars are twinkly and pretty.
   d) All of the above.
3. Did you enjoy guessing which member of the

away team on *Star Trek* was likely to be killed before the first commercial? Should he have consulted his horoscope before volunteering?

4. What do YOU think Cementhands meant when he called pufferfish "the piano movers of the sea"? Which of the following sounds most correct to you?
   a) Sea sponges are the "homeless guy with the squeegie" of the sea.
   b) Dolphins are the proctologists of the sea.
   c) Jellyfish are the ballerinas of the sea.
   d) You guys have spent way too much time at sea.
5. Who is the current deputy aide to the assistant deputy press secretary at the White House? How do you know? Did you check the stars, or Google?

Seaworthy— Capable of handling the sea and all its dangers. Is there a finer compliment from one nautical person to another? We thought not.

Seven Seas— Don't get caught in the trap of trying to name the Seven Seas. It's a sucker bet. "Uh, the Caribbean. The Mediterranean . . . uh . . ." There aren't seven in particular. The Seven Seas means all the oceans of the world. Trying to name them identifies you quickly as a lubber who has no business talking like a pirate.

17
Cap'n Slappy's Practical Parrot Pointers

Cap'n Slappy is to advice columns what food poisoning is to a weight-loss plan—yes, it can get the job done, but it's messy, dangerous and not really the tool you wanted at all. Yet "Ask Cap'n Slappy" has become the most popular fixture of our Web site, much to the

Shark bait— A person who's been thrown overboard without benefit of a life jacket, because they will presumably be eaten by sharks. In point of fact, sharks rarely attack people. You'd be far more likely to drown, which in the end probably isn't any more fun but is far more accurate. If truth be told, you'd probably end up as rotting bits of crab bait. But in the vernacular, accuracy is often tossed overboard in the name of being colorful, so "shark bait" it is.

chagrin of Ol' Chumbucket, who thought his stamp-collecting column would be the big draw. Cap'n Slappy is just like Ann Landers or Dear Abby, if either of those two good women were an irresponsible, flatulent drunkard with a obsession for weapons and flogging.

At www.talklikeapirate.com, Cap'n Slappy provides answers on any topic under the sun, anything that readers choose to ask. As we culled through the archives to prepare this chapter, we were surprised to learn just how many of those questions had to do with parrots.

Cap'n Slappy is NOT a licensed veterinarian. He is not even an enthusiastic layman with a love of animals. He doesn't actually have any pets and isn't allowed any under the terms of his probation—ever since "the goat incident," as the local constabulary still calls it. So with that warning out in the open, here's some of Slappy's advice on the pirate's flamboyantly colorful friend (we're talking parrots, not Richard Simmons).

Ahoy Thar Cap'n Slappy!

Me parrot, Cap'n Long John, keeps a-crappin' on me shoulder. What be the best way to get me pirate overcoat clean and fresh smellin'?

Arrr Thar, Poopsie Pirate!

Here's what ye do! Wrap yon parrot in plastic wrap. Superheat in the galley's hottest oven. Place back on shoulder. Use staples if necessary. Now that be yer poopless plastic pirate parrot!

CAP'N SLAPPY

Dear Cap'n Slappy,

Please help me. My husband refuses to paper-train his parrot. Any suggestions?

SAUCY WENCH (AKA RED)

Dear Saucy the Red,

In addition to a nice thick plastic coating on the bird (see earlier response), let me suggest this method of paper-training a parrot that was developed in Sweden by a team of Hungarian behaviorists who fancy a bit of parrot training when they are visiting Sweden.

1—Place the parrot on the paper and give the command, "Polly take a poopie."

2—Repeat until parrot poopies on the paper.

3—If after several attempts the parrot refuses to poopie on the paper, shake your hook in the parrot's face in a menacing gesture.

4—If the parrot leaves the paper and poopies elsewhere, hit it in the head with your hook, purchase a new parrot, place it on the paper and give the command, "Polly take a poopie."

The behaviorists have not yet reached an agreement about leaving the corpse of your

Morgan Adams
Status: Fictional
Buckle: Swashed
Vehicle: Movie, *Cutthroat Island*
Hotness factor: Very

Geena Davis played pirate captain Morgan Adams in *Cutthroat Island* and—Yes, we can hear you now: "But wait, Geena Davis is . . . a girl!" Let's just say we know this. Not a girl, actually—a woman, and a damn fine one at that. One who proved you can have good legs and still sack and pillage with the best of 'em. Aye, she's one wench who could join our crew any day. We can also hear you coughing politely and pointing out that, Geena's finer points aside, *Cutthroat Island* is not a particularly good movie. No, sadly, it pretty much bites. But Geena is fine in it. She's a salty wench and swashbuckles with the best of them.

last bird on the paper for the new bird as a little "lesson."

I hope that helps.

CAP'N SLAPPY

Do you have to have a parrot to be a pirate or talk like one??

Ahoy, Parrot-head!

It's Talk Like a **PIRATE** Day, not Talk Like a **PARROT** Day! The parrot is as much a part of Talk Like a Pirate Day as it would be at a Jimmy Buffet concert—nice set dressing, but it doesn't make the songs any sweeter! The best parrots are the stuffed/dead ones, unless you like to dress in newsprint.

Could you imagine Talk Like a Parrot Day? People would be gutting each other in the streets. "STOP REPEATING WHAT I SAY IN THAT HIGH NASAL VOICE, YOU #*#@($)#@!!!" people would say just before slicing you open with their cutlass.

Now, if you have a parrot, that's great! Treat them with care and they will be great gifts for your great-grandchildren, but for the love of Neptune, leave them in their cages on September 19. And for Jimmy's sake, don't take them to the concert!

CAP'N SLAPPY

Why do pirates like parrots?

PARROTBOY

Shiver me timbers— When the wind blows, when the gale is at full force, or when the enemy's broadsides are striking with alarming accuracy, the pirates' ship shudders so strongly that the very timbers may be said to shiver. Thus the phrase. It's used in the same sense as "blow me down," an expression of surprise, even incredulity or alarm. Interestingly, timbers appear to be the only thing that can be shivered. We've never heard, for instance, a person say "Shiver me yardarm" or "Shiver me chum." It just doesn't work. Timbers could almost be defined as "the things that are shivered."

Oh, how innocent you are, little Parrot-boy.

It's not that pirates like parrots. Parrots are drawn to pirates like barnacles are drawn to rocks. They just kind of stick there and get fed. That's it. No big mystery. Now, go read a book about dolphins.

CAP'N SLAPPY

Arrrr, Cap'n Slappy, tell me, is a parrot really the best pet for a pirate? Also, do pirates use moisturizer? And finally, what do pirates eat for breakfast?

PETUNIA

Ahoy, me little Petunia!

So full of questions today, aren't we? Parrots are great pets for pirates. They're sassy, they perch nicely on the shoulder and if the ship is going down, they can just fly away. The downside, of course, is the pooping. That's why Cap'n Slappy always has one coat made of newsprint. I call it me Paper Parrot Pirate Peacoat. When it gets too heavy, I just fling it away and make a new one.

As for pirates using moisturizer, pirates are keen on slapping weasel grease to it and marching on. Weasel grease is an excellent moisturizer, but even more effective as a sunscreen. Another good moisturizer is schnauzer grease, but it is more expensive and should NEVER be worn in the sun.

As for breakfasts, they are as varied as

pirates themselves. Some buccaneers have chum biscuits and chum gravy; others like hardtack toast, while others eat seagull eggs. I like Lucky ChARRRRms because they really are magically delicious.

CAP'N SLAPPY

Skull and crossbones— You know what this is. It's the universal symbol of pirates. Also known as the Jolly Roger, it is the flag that really flew over many a pirate ship, and showed that the ship bearing down on the harmless prey would give or take no quarter.

Do I need a parrot?

MATHEW

Dear Mathew

Seriously? Is that how ye spell yer name? What, couldn't afford the other T, eh?

Smartly— Do something quickly. "Smartly, me lass," you might say when sending the waitress off for another round. She will be so impressed she might well spit in your beer.

To answer yer question, though, no, you don't NEED a parrot. Small shoulder animals are an accessory to the whole pirate look. I knew a pirate named Steve—not Mad Steve or Dread Pirate Steve or Yellowbeard Steve, but just Steve—and he had a dachshund named Frederic. There was another pirate named Alan. He tried to get everyone to call him Alan the Bastard, but we all knew his parents. Nice folks, from Liverpool. So we just called him Alan who wishes he could be called a Bastard. Anyway, he called Frederic "Freddy" once and Steve cut him to pieces and mailed them home to his mum.

A couple of pirates tried to refer to Steve as "Cutter" after that, but he cut them to ribbons as well and mailed them home to their parents. Apparently, Steve and Frederic weren't into pirate nicknames.

But no, you don't need a parrot. But if you want a nickname, that might be nice.

CAP'N SLAPPY

Have you and your bird had intimate relations?

WICCER

Dear Wiccer,

No, but we do have intimidating relations. Expect a visit from one of them soon.

CAP'N SLAPPY

Where can I buy a parrot?

PARROTLESS IN PEORIA

Dear Peon,

"Bought" parrots are so gauche. It is always best when a parrot chooses YOU. Do like I do: Stand alone, naked, in a tropical jungle, and recite Shakespearean sonnets until a beautiful plumed friend lands on your shoulder. THIS will be your parrot friend for life, because it has chosen you. Remember to check for lice (this is where having a ship's monkey comes in handy).

If that fails, you can always pick up a bird at Papa Paulo's Parrot Pavilion in Pottsville, Pennsylvania (monkey not included).

CAP'N SLAPPY

Spanish Main— The coastal region of Spanish America in the sixteenth and seventeenth centuries. It spread roughly from the Isthmus of Panama to the mouth of the Orinoco River in Venezuela. (OK, we admit it. We looked that one up.)

Spar— A wooden or metal pole attached to the mast to support a sail. In other words, the sideways parts sticking out from the mast.

Arrrr! Avast, Cap'n Slappy. Does ye know where the treasure of the Sierra Madre be buried? If ye don't tell me its whereabouts, I'll have to swing ye from the yardarm, matey.

Dear Me Questionaire,

Cap'n Slappy loves these kinds of trick questions. It's like the old "Who is buried in Grant's tomb?" or "What is the difference in weight between a pound of gold and a pound of goose feathers?" Well, the way I sees it, Sierra Madre means something about "mountain mama" which was a line in a John Denver song, and he was singing about West Virginia. Therefore, this would lead me to believe that the treasure of the Sierra Madre was buried with John Denver.

Now, whar did I put me shovel?

CAP'N SLAPPY

(Ol' Chumbucket adds: There IS in fact a difference between the weight of a pound of gold and a pound of feathers, because one—gold, he's pretty sure—is measured in troy ounces and the other is measured in a scale with an odd-sounding name like Arnold. Unfortunately for the purposes of this question, he's not certain which is heavier. He thinks it's a pound of feathers, but wouldn't swear to it. Both Cap'n Slappy and Ol' Chumbucket assume ye're speakin' here of parrot feathers.)

Dear Cap'n Slappy,

I have just come into possession of an old treasure map. The previous owner mysteriously disappeared before finding the treasure. Because of this I think it would be a prudent business move to purchase the real estate under the X. Do you know of any competent realtors with experience in this sort of transaction?

TYCOON CORSAIR

Dear Mr. Corsair,

I used to know of a realtor who handled transactions like that, but I buried him under an X. Remember, when making any real estate purchase, the three rules are: "Location, location, and don't piss off a pirate!"

CAP'N SLAPPY

Dear Cap'n Slappy,

During a recent encounter with a scurvy knave of a swashbuckler my arm was detached below the elbow. My question: How much time do I have to get it reattached?

SLEEVELESS IN SEATTLE

Dear Sleeveless,

If you're in Seattle, I can "hook" you up with a guy I know. Mad Jaime's Hooks and Pegs is one of the finest places I know to go for that custom-built hook or that specialty peg. It's located there on the waterfront in the basement of Ye Olde Curiosity Shoppe (the basement is only open when the tide is

WAY out). Keep the arm, though. Mad Jaime will take it as a trade-in.

CAP'N SLAPPY

Ahoy, Cap'n!

Does your bandana make your head look fat?

JOKEY LEGLESS

Dear Legoless,

No. My HUGE head, which is of legendary size—much larger, in fact, than any other human head—makes my head look fat. Also, foods from the golden brown food group contribute to the fatness of my head.

Thanks for asking.

CAP'N SLAPPY

What is the best type of sword for a pirate?

BLOODGUTS THE WRETCHED

Dear Wretch,

As me sainted Granny McCafferty used to say, "A rapier may be witty, but a cutlass makes 'em gutless!" And then she beat me with a stick. I miss me granny!

CAP'N SLAPPY

Arrr, Cap'n,

Do ye like ta bury bones with yer treasure? Makes the scallywags shiver their timbers as they're discoverin' yer booty.

CAP'N GRAYBEARD

Spitten image— Everyone says this wrong. Everyone says a person who looks like someone else is the "spitting" image. Well, it's got nothing to do with expectorating. Nothing. The bowsprit, or part of the ship which extends out in front, is also sometimes called the spit. Here you will often find a carved figurehead, which sometimes was such a good likeness that it bore an uncanny resemblance to the person it represented. Someone who bears an uncanny resemblance to another person is as like to that person as a spit. Hence, spitten image.

Ahoy, Graybeard!

Believe you me, many a scallywag has had his timbers shivered when he discovered MY booty! And that's WITHOUT me burying any bones in it! But then, Cap'n Slappy has an AMAZING booty and he is very selective about where he buries his bones.

CAP'N SLAPPY

Hello, Captain,

How'd you get that hook on your hand?

DAVE

Ahoy, Dave!

Thar be a story thar, but first, I must point out that I didn't get a hook "on" me hand. If I had a hand, I wouldn't need a hook, now would I? How do I get it on me stump of a wrist? It's a screw-in. Cap'n Slappy has other attachments as well, but he is fond of his hook.

If ye want to know how I lost me hand, let me just point out that thar be a reason they have outlawed drunken underwater shark boxing. But, alas, it came too late for Ol' Cap'n Slappy.

Well, it's time to brush me tooth. Now, whar did I put me hook brush?

CAP'N SLAPPY

How does this work?

CONFUSED

Spyglass— A telescope, usually one that can be comfortably held in the hands, making it not much use for actually looking at faraway things while standing on a heaving quarterdeck.

Stow— Put away. You can use it in the sense of "stop that" or "shut up." "Stow that talk, ya bilge rat."

Ahoy, Confused,

I am not sure how it works for you, but some people hold it off to the side and shake it. Others move it back and forth in front of them vigorously. Some hold it high above their head and let it just kind of do its own thing. Still others feel the need to strike it or hit it against something, often their own body.

Look, it isn't that confusing. Tambourines are fun and easy to play.

CAP'N SLAPPY

Where do pirates go to the restroom on their ships? Do they use the poop deck? Doesn't it get smelly with all that excess pirate waste?

POOPER THE PIRATE

Arrr, ye little Pooper!

Here be some little-known facts about piratoilets.

- Some pirate ships come with a toilet—we seafaring types call it a "head."
- A French pirate named Pierre Bartée perfected the art of positioning himself off the back of the ship so that he could go when he needed to. His contortions were thought to be not only artistic but scientific as well, and a little platform was built off of the poop deck to accommodate him. As his shipmates watched, they studied his moves until "Le Bartée" became synony-

mous with the seagoing equivalent of the rest area.

- When he went to build his pirate ship, the infamous Stede Bonnet was asked by the shipmaster if he wanted the more expensive head built on his ship, or just a Le Bartée. Not one to make a snap decision, Bonnet replied, "Oh, just give me Le Bartée OR give me head."
- After some unsuccessful weeks as a pirate, Stede Bonnet was hanged.

Now, if you ask ANY expert about this, they will tell you Cap'n Slappy is all wrong! That's why these are LITTLE KNOWN facts.

CAP'N SLAPPY

Pirate Philosophy

What is the meaning of life?

ZACH

Arrrr, little Zach,

This is a question that has perplexed the greatest minds of human history. Therefore, it is no problem to explain. Life is something that happens to people who aren't burdened by the need to find meaning in everything. Now go out and do some wenching!

CAP'N SLAPPY

Swab— Mop, as in "Swab the deck!" Certainly other things could be swabbed, but in our minutes of intensive research we don't recall ever hearing of anyone swabbing anything else. Still, good pirate verbs are hard to come by. A swab or swabby is also a less than complimentary way to refer to a sailor, the indication being that all he is good for is mopping up after the "real" pirates have done the hard work.

Why do these things keep happening?

BAFFLED BUCCANEER

Dear Baffy Buc,

Rather than boring you with the ins and outs of quantum mechanics, let me just explain that these "things" don't keep happening. These "events" keep happening. For instance, you might hear one of your friends say, "Dude, I got tickets to the concert of our most favorite rock and roll hippity hop band! It will be the schnizzizle on my nizzle." At this point, it will be important to strike your friend hard upon his head with a blunt object—say, a belaying pin, a rock or a petrified weasel. But back to the point, this concert will be an "event," not a "thing"!

People say, "I am going to the concert event of the century!" People don't say, "I am going to the concert thing of the thingy," unless they have severe petrified weasel trauma to the prefrontal lobe.

So Cap'n Slappy did extensive research on this, which means I called my friend, Joe Don, who works for "Events International." You may have seen him at any number of music or World Wrestling Entertainment events. He was wearing a bright yellow jacket that read EVENT STAFF. I asked Joe Don, "Why do events keep happening?" and he said, "Because they need to keep the stadium booked!"

So there is your answer, Baffy. These "things," as you put them, keep happening because they need to keep the stadium booked.

Good question!

CAP'N SLAPPY

why am i so smart?

KATIE H

Dear Katie,

If you actually were so smart, you'd know why.

CAP'N SLAPPY

I really really need to know who would win in a streetfight: Shrek or the Incredible Hulk?

PEGLEG JACKSON

Dear Peggy,

Shrek is very strong and fights well. When he is joined by Donkey they form a formidable duo. The Incredible Hulk, on the other hand, is . . . well . . . "incredible." Now, a streetfight has no rules and victory may go to the fighter with the most creativity. Shrek, being a funny fellow, shows loads of creativity, and that Donkey is hilarious! Still, the Incredible Hulk has that whole incredible thing going for him.

So here's how it breaks down scientifically. The Incredible Hulk being so incredible, will smash lovable Shrek with one blow and then wipe his incredible bottom with Donkey. You can bank on it!

Now, where is Don King to promote this?

CAP'N SLAPPY

Dear Cap'n Slappy,

Why does the porridge bird lay its egg in the air?

BLACKBREAD

Dear "Blackbread,"

They are showing off. Just ignore them and they will stop.

CAP'N SLAPPY

If violence isn't the answer, why does it always work?

JAKIE FIRECRACKER, DAS COMMANDANT AND OBERFUHRER OF THE ANTIREALITY, PHFRYKI CHYCK #1, PROFESSIONAL OTAKU, SHE WHO DRIVES THREADS OFF-TOPIC, ETC. ETC.

Dear Etc.,

Who said violence isn't the answer? Oh, wait. Maybe I DID say that in one of my pacifist moods. Alright, NEW rule! Violence is NOT the answer unless it's going to work better than nonviolence, and the best judge of that be ME! In future, all violence must be cleared by Cap'n Slappy and reviewed by the

Swashbuckler— One who engages in showy heroics; also, movies and books featuring such characters. The all-time great swashbuckler was Errol Flynn, the star of *The Sea Hawk* and *Captain Blood*, two of the best pirate movies ever made. The true swashbuckler performs his dangerous deeds with a brio and savoir faire that make the risk of his life seem a matter of no consequence. It's all a question of style. It has been pointed out to us by the persnickety that you can swash your buckle, but you cannot buckle your swash, because your buckle is a shield (isn't "sword and buckler" a biblical phrase? We should probably know that). And swashing it means clashing it in a loudly fierce way to frighten the enemy before engaging him or her in combat. And that's more than we ever wanted to know about the subject.

Committee of Violent Decision-Making appointed by Cap'n Slappy. Damn! Bylaws are tough!

CAP'N SLAPPY

(Ol' Chumbucket adds: Whoever said violence isn't the answer didn't ask the right question.)

Dear Cap'n Slappy

Why?

WONDERING

Dear Wondering,

What a thoughtful question. You know, I think it was me sainted Granny McCafferty who summed up the answer to "why" better than anyone I have ever known or ever will know.

One time, when I was a tyke, Granny McCafferty asked me to stop strangling her little poodle, Tippy. When I asked, "Why?" she said, "Because I said so." Then she beat me with a stick.

Now, are you gonna get all sassmouth with Cap'n Slappy and his granny?

CAP'N SLAPPY

Dear Cap'n Slappy,

Ahoy, dear Slappy! Last weekend I gradumatated from the illustrious University of Oregon in Philosophy and Sociology, and suddenly have doubts about my scholastic career. Should I

Swing the lead— Sailors measured the distance to the bottom by throwing out a measured line with a lead weight. Knowing how far it is to the seafloor or a coral reef is important if you don't want the bottom ripped out of your ship. That could be embarrassing to any pirate. Now they have sonar and other electronic gizmos, but swinging the lead is a more time-honored phrase. Use it when you're trying to determine a distance.

have studied swashbuckling and chumswilling instead?

SEAMAN SEMEN

Dear Seaman Duck Semen,

It is a sad day for edumacation everywhere when a Philosophy and Sociology major did not at least get the sense that he was also gradumatating with a Life Studies degree in buckling the ol' swash and swilling the ol' chum! Ol' Chumbucket has a son who also gradumatated from Oregon with a similar set of albatrosses around his academic neck. But like you, he will be just fine.

Mad Jack Redbeard, Cap'n Slappy's nephew and Ol' Chumbucket's boy, and you and the thousands like you who are entering the job market with your little tadpole tails flicking as you approach the big egg of happiness will look back in fond memory of your college days and realize, "I should have gone to Europe and gotten laid."

CAP'N SLAPPY

Dear Cap'n Slappy
Will you help me?

JULIE

Ahoy, Julie!

Of course I will help you! Cap'n Slappy is here for you! He loves you and wants to help you in any way he can. Do you need a shoulder to cry on? Cap'n Slappy is here to help. Do you need a cheating boyfriend beaten senseless and tossed, bound and gagged, onto a ship bound for Bangladesh? Cap'n Slappy is here to help. Do you need the kind of lovin' that only an old sea dog can give? Cap'n Slappy is always here to help. Do you need help moving? Cap'n Slappy is going to be out of town that weekend, but be sure to let him know NEXT time you move.

There is nothing that Cap'n Slappy wouldn't pretend to be willing to do for you, Julie.

That's just the kind of Pirate Guy Cap'n Slappy is.

CAP'N SLAPPY

Ummm, I don't mean to be rude, but what gives you the authority to give advice? Aren't you a beer-swilling pirate guy with no manners?

SNOOTY PETUNIA IN TEXAS

Dear Snotty,

Like most people who "don't mean to be rude," your penchant for accidental rudeness is matched only by your ability to get it "wrong" with such regularity one can only imagine that you are the Metamucil of wrongness. My "authority" to give unbridled advice all willy-nilly comes via a mandate from Great Neptune himself. Also, I have a master's degree in Buttinsky Studies (MBS)

Tales, dead men tell no— Blackbeard was the pirate credited with the practice of taking his treasure ashore with a single sailor, burying it, then killing his assistant and throwing him in the hole before covering it up. That way he would be the only one who knew precisely where the treasure was hidden. We presume that after the first few times Blackbeard and a sailor rowed ashore to bury treasure and ol' Teach came back alone, the rest of the crew figured out this was not a good shore duty to be volunteering for.

from that illustrious paragon of higher edumacation, Porkland State University.

As for being a "beer-swilling pirate guy with no manners," alright, I am that. So, you got one right! But even a broken clock is correct twice a day.

Cordially,

CAP'N SLAPPY

Ginger or Mary Ann? I just can't decide.

GILLIGAN, MATE ABOARD THE MINNOW

Ahoy, little buddy!

Here be the deal. Many a philosopher has lost sleep over the much-talked-about "Ginger versus Mary Ann" debate. Nietzsche fancied Mary Ann, while Descartes was all about Ginger. Plato couldn't keep his mind off of the Professor. But none of that matters to a willowy little wisp of a lad such as yerself, who has had the fortune of being marooned with two women who wouldn't give him the time of day on the mainland if he set himself on fire and sang "I've Got a Loverly Bunch of Coconuts"!

Still, thar ye be. Two lovely and varied beauties and you are trying to "decide"? What's the matter with ye? One of you, two of them, Skipper's impotent and the Professor is obsessed with building a radio out of coconuts. Hell, the wenches would tag-team ye just to keep ye from ruining their chance of being rescued every week.

Gilligan, ye must learn to play the hand ye're dealt. And lad, ye've been dealt a full house!

CAP'N SLAPPY

18

A True Story of Pirattitude in Action

In Which we relate an absolutely true story (really, it's true!) as a model for how the aspiring pirate can become a role model for a whole community.

Alright, lads and lasses! Gather around and let's raise a cup in honor of the American Pirate Association in, of all places, Holland, Michigan. Not the sort of place you'd expect to find a lot of pirates, but these lads have done the cause proud, and no mistake.

What you're about to read is absolutely true. It's the only chapter in this whole book in which we pledge without reservation that we're not making this up. It's backed up by newspaper stories from the Holland (Michigan) *Sentinel*, along with actual interviews conducted by yours truly. Yes! We actually stirred off our behinds to ferret out the details of this remarkable true story because . . . well, because it's a remarkable story and it's true. Now sit quietly and stop askin' foolish questions while we tell it, or it's belayin' pins to the noggins for all of ye wee rascals. And fetch us a tot of rum so our throats don't dry out. There's a good pirate. Now, on with the story.

Once upon a time there was a town in Michigan that held an annual Tulip Time Festival each spring, because they're all good-natured Dutch people who have a lot of tulips up there and some extra time on their hands. The festival features three parades, including—and this is the important one to the story—the Kinderparade.

Now, you'd think the children's Kinderparade would be for the children, and you'd be right, more or less. More than seven thousand kids take part, mostly in adorable little Dutch boy and girl costumes, clomping down the street in their cute little wooden shoes. That's a lot of adorable kids.

Mary Read
Dude name: Mark Read
Difference between Real and Fake Name: K/Y—easy to remember. Easy to insert rude joke here—made easier with lubrication.
Hobbies: Disguising herself as a man, piracy, collecting unicorns
Once again, perhaps too much has been made of Cap'n Slappy's unnatural obsession with the Bonney–Read connection, but it only seems fair to hear his side of the story, over and over and over again. But it must be stated that she was a fierce fighter. Her husband was once challenged to a duel, and Mary was so certain he'd be killed that she took his place and killed the opponent. She and her quite possibly hot, perhaps lesbian, partner Anne Bonney staved off the attack of the British authorities and avoided the gallows by "pleading their bellies." Of course, no births were ever recorded, but the prison inventory indicated that two pillows were missing from C Block. Clever lesbians.

Treasure— Call it booty, call it plunder, call it what you will, this is what being a pirate is all about. That and the accessories.

But don't for a minute let yourself think that just because it's the children's parade that the children have any actual control. They're really just props. The parade is closely monitored by the Tulip Time Festival board, which is made up of many hardworking Dutch enthusiast volunteers and by, as it turns out, the local police. The way it works is, each elementary school is assigned a theme relating to their Dutch heritage. The only other participants are the local marching bands and sometimes the sponsor of that particular parade. They don't accept any outside applications for the Kinderparade.

A group of high school students wanted to take part in the fun, but they didn't have the proper permit. Calling themselves the American Pirate Association, they dressed up in pirate garb and showed up in 2003, where they were "not so politely asked to leave," as one of their number related to us. So they went to a nearby park and amused themselves and some of the festival's thousands of tourists by conducting a pirate battle. Under the rules, anyone who was "stabbed" had to lie on the ground for two minutes before rejoining the fray. For those watching it must have been like a cross between *Pirates of the Caribbean* and *Night of the Living Dead*, the park littered with bodies that would periodically rise and begin battling again.

They planned to reenact the battle in 2004, but something came up. This time the group didn't try to go to the parade staging area and ask if they could take part. Instead, they waited until the parade was under way and jumped in en route. As luck would have it, they were right behind the local bank's float, which seemed appropriate for pirates. They carried a banner declaring their group's name and flew a Jolly Roger borrowed from a teacher.

They were rather surprised that the brazen tactic worked, because there they were in the parade and getting away with it. People applauded and waved and cheered—for a while. Then they were found out, and the police, taking a "zero tolerance" stance, removed them from the parade.

When the officer moved in, most of the pirates broke ranks and ran, leaping through the densely packed crowd of onlookers. The officer nabbed two of them, and got the names of others. Each of the nineteen kids was cited for illegal entry into a parade route and fined $100.

A hundred bucks a head for crashing a parade. Wow! That's some serious shit, especially when you consider these are first-time parade crashers. But the Holland authorities, hereinafter collectively referred to as "The Man," weren't going to stand for any such misbehavior from the town's youth.

The kids, God love 'em, didn't complain. These were not "bad" kids, not slackers or stoners with skateboards and surly attitudes, listening to the grinding, angry music of disaffected youth gone rancid. No, even The Man conceded that point. One of the kids was the class president; another was the vice president. Many of them were honor students. One of them is, at this writing, a cadet at

Three sheets to the wind— Extremely drunk. The sheets are the ropes that adjust the position of the sails to the wind. If the sheets are broken or loose, the sails will thrash wildly and the ship will be difficult to control, a prey to the wind. The ship will lurch drunkenly. Typically a sailing ship would have three masts, and if the sheets to all three were damaged, the ship would be almost impossible to control. Much like your brother-in-law when he's had too much to drink.

West Point. Not only were they not stoners, dropouts, disc jockeys and the like; they were arguably among the best kids the community had to offer.

"It was reasonable to ticket us," said Tom Morkes, the pirate who is now a cadet. "But $100 was too much. I think they're a little uptight at Tulip Time."

The Man was unbending. To those of us "of an age," we know this is The Man's way of keeping a brother down.

"If we allow this to occur, there's no doubt we'll see more of it next year," Holland Chief of Police John Kruithoff said in the newspaper story detailing what happened. "We're not going to condone any of this type of behavior."

Remember, "zero tolerance" means "zero thought." Rigidity means never having to say "I'm thinking."

In fairness, The Man had a point. It's not like the authorities were being totally unreasonable. Chief Kruithoff (a surprisingly reasonable fellow when not in The Man mode) told us over the phone that he had two concerns. The first was that there are three high schools in the area. The American Pirate Association represents students from one of those schools. If they had "gotten away with it," Kruithoff feared that the following year another school would try to top them, and the thing would escalate into a growing series of parade pranks. This is what experts in the law enforcement field call the Slippery Slope of Prankish Piratical Pugnacity. And that, from The Man's point of view, is a bad thing. The other concern was that the kids' entrance and exit from the parade was made through a dense crowd, and somebody could get hurt. Okay, we'll give him that one.

So the fine was a hundred bucks a head, and the chief told us if they did it again, the fine would be higher the next year.

The next Monday, back at school, the halls were buzzing with reports of what had happened in the parade. A teacher, grinning, talked about making a banner for the classroom that would say HOME OF THE AMERICAN PIRATE ASSOCIATION. But then, one by one, the nineteen students began getting called into the office. According to Jon Fegel, one of the pirates called in by The Man, "A lot of the office people were talking in pirate voices as well when I was called down to meet with the principal. I was sent home for improper use of school materials—I had printed off pirate flyers and handed them out to people at school. But it was said that the assistant principal was speaking like a pirate the rest of the day."

Now, here's the part where the story rises from the status of a fun yarn and takes on mythic proportions. The kids had to come up with a total of $1,900. They didn't want to ask their parents for it, and they didn't want to get jobs so close to the end of the school year. And knocking over a liquor store was definitely out of the question. They're *good* kids, remember. So they did what many a high school throughout this great land has done. They held a car wash. It was a benefit for the American Pirate Association. Dressed like pirates,

Weigh anchor— Raise the anchor and store it so you can be on your way. As you rise from the table where you've been celebrating Talk Like a Pirate Day say, "Well, mateys, time for me to weigh anchor."

Wench— A saucy woman, typically of a lower class—barmaids, actresses, that sort of thing. It used to mean a young woman, plain and simple. But try explaining that to the woman who works in the next cubicle when she takes offense at your use of the word. The word "wench" works best with spicy-tasting modifiers, including the word "spicy" itself. Think about it—"spicy wench," "saucy wench," "sweet wench," "tart wench."

they got hoses and buckets and soap and set out to raise the money they needed to pay their debt to their Tulip Time–loving society.

How did the community react to these miscreants? We'll let Holland *Sentinel* reporter Richard Harrold tell the story, as it appeared in the paper the next day.

> *Customers were already showing up Saturday morning for a car wash before it was even set up to raise money for a group of teens who were fined $100 each for jumping uninvited into a Tulip Time parade.*
>
> *More than enough money was collected—some customers didn't even want their car washed and just drove by to leave money . . . They collected nearly $400 in their first hour of operation . . .*
>
> *Larry Schutte of Hamilton was one of the teens' first customers. He'd been following the story of the American Pirate Association—the group's name—in the local media.*
>
> *"It wasn't any major problem what they did," Schutte said. "I know they* [the city and Tulip Time: eds.—The Man] *had to set an example. You can't have people jumping into parades like that, but the $100 seemed a bit steep. They seem like really good kids . . ."*
>
> *The group had no set fee for the car wash. Customers were as generous as they cared to be. One customer paid $60 for his car wash. Some even showed up wearing a little pirate spirit of their own. Al Davis and Deb Wiersma, both of Holland, showed up on their motorcycles dressed in*

pirate attire. Flying on a long pole from the back of Davis' Harley-Davidson was a Jolly Roger. He was sporting a faux parrot on his shoulder, an eye patch and a tricorner hat.

When the students saw Davis and Wiersma arrive, a chorus of cheers and "Yarr, matey!" erupted.

"We came out to support the pirates," Davis said.

The teacher who wanted to put up a banner stopped to deliver doughnuts he'd gotten a local bakery, Marge's, to donate.

In all, the kids raised more than enough to pay their fines. There was $500 left over. What to do with the remainder?

The city of Holland was building a new police station, and was taking donations. They wanted to erect a statue of a police officer holding a little kid by the hand, the chief said. Anyone donating $100 to the statue would get his or her name engraved in a brick to be placed in the rotunda. The members of the American Pirate Association decided to donate the extra money to the fund in return for a brick with the group's name on it. They made a peace offering to The Man.

And that's where the story should end, but of course it doesn't. Because The Man refused the money. He didn't want peace with the pirates. The Man is only comfortable with conflict and control. Damn! The Man sucks!

Chief Kruithoff told us he would have accepted the money if the inscription was for the high

West Indies— The islands separating the Caribbean Sea from the Atlantic Ocean. These include the Bahamas and the Antilles (Greater and Lesser, although all the Antilles seem pretty great to us).

school's class for 2004—"I wouldn't have had a problem with that"—but not in the name of the American Pirate Association, because "it's a fictitious name."

C'mon! Even King George offered amnesty for pirates who gave up the trade and turned themselves in. And it's not like the kids were defiant or anything. They did it for a lark, took their punishment with humor and good grace, and tried to make amends. Amends apparently weren't wanted, so in the end the kids donated all $500 to the town's Boys and Girls Club. At least kids will benefit from that.

This would probably be an appropriate place to mention that not all authority figures are rigid and inflexible. Our friends number many school administrators, and more than a few police officers around the world take part in Talk Like a Pirate Day. We got an e-mail from one in England who spent the whole day talking like a pirate, even when he pulled people over. He even wrote up his reports in pirate jargon.

But some people can't unbend at all. They put on their authority when they put on their uniforms—police, doctor, foreman, nun, whatever—and feel if they relax their authority, even for a bit, it's the same as going naked or something.

In the end, that's probably the lesson to be taken from all this: Sometimes it seems like grown-ups are just dicks. Not all of them, but some. And there's not a lot you can do about it except not let them spoil your day, because even when they seem like dicks, they have their point, too. And a lot of others are cool enough to know that a little chaos and creativity is a sign that all is well in the community.

Now get us some more rum, lads. We're parched.

Other Examples of Pirattitude in Action

People all over the world have been moved by Talk Like a Pirate Day and the spirit behind it, pirattitude. Many of them have sent us photos and descriptions of their activities. We have seen photos of people sitting in a bank conference room, looking all businesslike except for the newspaper pirate hats they all wore. We've seen high school and college kids invading their campuses under the Jolly Roger. People on sailing ships, dressed as pirates. People at work, dressed as pirates. And, of course, people with their beloved dogs and cute little kittens dressed as pirates, so you can take this too far.

Here, selected at random, are a few reports fans have sent us of how they've celebrated Talk Like a Pirate Day.

Pirates in blue—*Ye'll be wantin' to know the swing shift pirates of the Manteca, California, Police Department have all adopted TLAPD. At the stroke of midnight a lonely pirate was calling out on the radio, "Manteca, there be an ill wind a-blowin' out here. Tell the citizens who call to be wary, 'cuz pirates are afoot!" One buccaneer was overheard telling a speeder,*

Yardarm— The yard was a long spar slung to the mast of a ship to support and spread the mainsail. The yardarm is either end of the yard, which could be used to hang things or winch them onto the ship. There was a rule in polite company that it wasn't proper to drink before the sun was over the yardarm—in other words, until afternoon. We've always felt, and pirates probably agreed, that if the sun wasn't over the yardarm, the only proper thing to do was move to the other side of the yardarm, check out the sun again, and then open the bottle.

"Ye'll be signin' in the red box, lassie!" Many fleet ships have been heard around town with mysterious voices on the PA systems singing "Yo HO, Yo HO, a pirate's life for me!" After a pursuit of a suspect driving a stolen motorcycle ended and we caught the suspect, someone asked me if the bad guy had asked for "parlay." I of course responded, "No. We brought the long guns to bear!" And of course when the drunk driver ran off the freeway, a passing pirate was heard over the PA system yelling, "MAN OVERBOARD!" We're using our pirate names today. You can imagine the looks on people's faces . . .

Casino pirates—*I'm a retired commercial deep-sea diver and certified USCG captain now working in the casino industry in Atlantic City, New Jersey . . . Myself and all of the personnel in the surveillance room did in fact observe Talk Like a Pirate Day. We enjoyed the entire day and were able to recruit several people to talk like a pirate all day.*

Better late than never—*My wife and I were married last year on September 20. We had a party the day before, and our friends, being who they are, were already talking like pirates when we arrived. Then they applied "it must still be September 19 SOMEWHERE" logic to carry Talk Like a Pirate Day over to September 20, and at our reception, a few of them donned pirate garb and attempted to make off with my bride. They were foiled, and we've now been happily married for a year.*

Welsh pirattitude—*I first heard about Talk Like a Pirate [Day] on BBC Radio 2 over here in Wales (UK) last year. I (Dastardly) Dave and my work colleague (Not So Jolly) Roger have since discussed it on* *several occasions and this year we decided to do something about it . . . To begin with we were just going to celebrate the day but people kept coming over to our section and asking what it was in aid of so we decided to collect money for charity. We had eye patches, tricorns, cutlasses, Jolly Rogers and lots of booty (hmmm). The treasure consisted of glazed sweets (precious stones), ship's biscuits (cookies), musket balls (small round chocolates called Maltesers over here) and antiscurvy supplies (fruit). Much fun was had and we raised some cash for charity.*

Pigeon Forge pirates—*Arr, we were in Pigeon Forge, Tennessee, for the anual Grand Rod Run, riding in the back of me best mate's truck. Alas, the schooner is not well suited for a long journey in such a fashion. Lo, the lower regions of me body were beginning to ache. Tho' his wench was quite irritated by me talking like a pirate for the day, aye, even she laughed at this: "GARRR, this truck be hurting me booty." Not only was there excess mirth, even the old sea hag herself let out an "ARRR" or three.*

On the way to the farrrrrrum—*Ahoy. We two wenches spent TLAPD at a local theater production of* A Funny Thing Happened on the Way to the Forum, *and had occasion to "Arrrrrr" when we were spotted in the audience during preshow announcements, wearing our pirate hats acquired at Long John Silver's, where we got some grub and grog before the show. During the production, every time the subplot about the twin babies kidnapped by pirates was mentioned, we waved our hats in the air from the back row. Arrr, it was an afternoon to remember.*

Never too young—*I just wanted to let you know*

that our two-year-old daughter named Trinity was born on International Talk Like a Pirate Day and we will be blending this theme with Dora the Explorer's Pirate Adventure Movie theme with an awesome array of decorations and games. We've even created an authentic pirate map (complete with blowtorch holes) with family-named islands and a big red treasure X mark for a pin-the-treasure-chest-on-the-X game. We will have Jolly Roger cake toothpicks, etc. So, thanks for the inspiration and know that there is at least one little birthday girl that will always celebrate ITLAP Day. Arrrrr!!!!

From Korea—*Last year, while in Korea (six kilometers south of North Korea on the DMZ), we had an entire cavalry troop talking like pirates. One of my soldiers kept talking about it for weeks before September 19. Pretty soon, everyone in our Scout platoon was anticipating the holiday by practicing his pirate talk. Well, the day finally arrived and we were preparing for our fall gunnery at the Korean Training Center, doing a testing phase called the BCPC. Nothing sounds more piratty than the letters BCPC spoken aloud with a heavy accent. Soon others outside of our platoon (namely people in charge) wanted to know exactly what the hell we were doing acting like fools with all the Arrrrs and such. Didn't take long for the explanation to make the rounds and soon our entire cavalry troop (C Troop, 4th Squadron 7th Cavalry Regiment GARRY OWEN!) was talking like pirates. We killed many targets with 25 MM Bushmaster Autocanon sabot and high explosive rounds that holiday.*

More pirates in uniform—*Just wanted to let you guys know that we are celebrating Talk Like a Pirate*

Ye—An archaic form of "you." We've seen people seriously overuse this one. A little ye goes a long way, so use it sparingly or ye might live to regret it.

Zanzibar—An island off the eastern coast of Africa. Use it in the sense of an exotic locale. "I'm off to Zanzibar," you might say when leaving for work. Or when leaving work.

Day here at the Intelligence Directorate (J-2), Special Operations Command Europe (SOCEUR), located in Stuttgart, Germany . . . We kinda started late, so there'll be no hats, eye patches or other necessary pirate gear. We have a few navy guys here in the office. Don't know if they'll participate. One of them says he won't because he's afraid he'd show us all up!! Arrr, he don't be knowing the first thing about piracy! I think even our boss (a full-fledged colonel) will be participating.

19

Life Aboard the *Festering Boil*

In Which the Pirate Guys completely lose it and begin making up their own sea saga.

So what was it really like to be a crew member of a buccaneering ship in the Golden Age of Pirates?

Why are you asking us? We'll say this one more time—this book is supposed to be sold in the humor section, not history. If you bought it thinking we actually know what we're talking about, well, we're sorry but that's really not our fault.

That is not to say we don't have our ideas. It's just that our picture of life on a pirate ship is mostly colored by Hollywood movies and our own fertile imaginations. And so, we'd guess, is yours, if you're anything like the vast majority of readers and unlike the small minority who take their pirate history seriously.

Here is an important point, so get out a pencil and paper and write this down. Actually, that seems silly, since it's already in this book. Anyway, here it is: Pirattitude is an attitude, a way of living your life, but it doesn't automatically convey any actual knowledge. If you want to become a 100 percent accurate pirate reenactor with the proper shoes and a greatcoat sewn with the proper stitching (and no cheating and using artificial fabrics) that's gonna take some work. And you should know how we feel about that by now.

What you have here is make-believe pirates basing their nautical daydreams on cheap celluloid. We'd as easily tell you what it was like on the set of an Errol Flynn or Tyrone Power swashbuckler movie. The problem for those who like strict accuracy (and what are you doing here if you do?) is those movies rarely if ever depict day-to-day life on the ship. It's all battles and broadsides and swinging from the rigging with a knife clenched in your teeth. Sure, that's very cool, but what happens the day before, or—God help us—two weeks

Captain Jack Sparrow
Status: Fictional
Location of operations: The Caribbean
Ship name: The *Black Pearl*
Ship status: Cursed
Excuse for misbehavior: "Pirate!?"
Captain Jack Sparrow was brought to life by the considerable acting talents of Johnny Depp. He is the embodiment of all of the swashbuckling hero pirates the cinema has offered in the past—from Errol Flynn to Tyrone Power and Burt Lancaster, with an extra helping of rock star Keith Richards thrown in for good measure. And we have it on good authority that the ladies find him to be quite attractive. His dogged determination to reclaim the *Black Pearl* shows the true spirit of pirattitude and the pure love that's possible between a man and an inanimate object, in this case a ship, even when it's cursed by the undead. For a contemporary comparison, you'd have to look at the love of a man for his pickup.

after a sea battle, with no action or port o' call in sight?

If we look at what are purported to be the journals of our old shipmate Edward Teach (better known to history, of course, as Blackbeard) we can get some idea.

"Such a day, Rum all out—Our Company somewhat sober—A damn'd confusion amongst us!—Rogues a-plotting—great Talk of Separation. So I look'd sharp for a Prize—such a Day took one, with a great deal of Liquor on board, so kept the Company hot, damn'd hot, then all Things went well again." (Quoted in *A General History of Pyrates,* written in 1724 by either Daniel Defoe or Captain Charles Johnson or—just possibly—William Shakespeare.)

Besides admiring Teach's piquant punctuation and creative composition, we can see that, to Blackbeard, the essential question was the same as it was almost three centuries later to actor Johnny Depp in *Pirates of the Caribbean* when he asked, "Why is the rum gone?"

But we can see that during those slack periods of pirating, time may have hung heavy over a crew, and it was a quick-witted captain's best course to keep the sailors busy and distracted or, when all else failed, drunk.

So, as long as we all understand where this is coming from, let's proceed to look at:

A Day Aboard the *Festering Boil*

Cap'n Slappy's ship's log:

Morning watch (8 a.m.)—Crew stirring. Wish they'd just stay in their hammocks, as there's not much for them to do today. We've done all the scut work and the crew is dangerously idle and sober. Asked Lt. Keeling to organize some activities, but all he's come up with for today is a spelling bee and a shufflefish tournament. Oh well, even if the lad can't keep the crew happy, he can at least keep 'em off my back and outta my hair. Think I'll join Ol' Chumbucket, who's sprawled out on the quarterdeck in his recliner with his morning mug o'ale.

Forenoon watch (Noon)—Keeling had to break out the cat-o'-nine-tails. Just brandishing it while saying uncomplimentary things about the sailors' mothers was enough to put down the threatened mutiny, but it was still a close thing. The spelling bee was less than successful at distracting the crew, especially since Cementhands McCormack is the only one with any schooling and he couldn't spell "dog" if one bit him on the ass. (Additional note: he cannot spell "ass" either.) Chumbucket recommends an early grog ration. I know I could go for one. So I think I will.

Dogwatch (6 p.m.)—Crew finished the last of the rum. There's been nary a sail on the horizon this fortnight, and if we don't find some prey soon I fear the crew could get ugly. Keeling trying to organize a sing-along. I can hear him trying to get the men to join him in a medley of show tunes. Blast his spirit and indomitableness. ("Indomitableness"? Hmmm. Good word—if it IS a word.)

Evening watch (8 p.m.)—The murmur of rebellion among the crew is growing so loud it's difficult to think. Or is that Chumbucket's snoring? Hard to tell. Sent down to Sawbones Burgess to release the supply of medicinal alcohol for the crew's late-night binge, but he says it's long gone and would some weasel grease do instead? I wonder what medical college he got his degree from, especially since it'll be another two hundred years before the requirements are standardized.

Midnight watch (12 a.m.)—Trouble narrowly averted when Dogwatch Watts managed to talk Cementhands out of his three kegs of a liquid he insists is something called "Chartreuse," but I remain dubious. It is a pungent yellowish liquid that makes the paint scream and bubble when inadvertently spilt. But the lads seemed happy enough and proceeded to get blissfully inebriated and have long since put themselves abed. When I asked the big man about his supply of such rare liquor, he assured me that he was well-connected to the source and that "the supply is inexhaustible." Then he offered me a tot and I declined politely. He said, "Well, Cap'n, just remember that anytime you want in to the Chartreuse Club, you're in!" Then he laughed his maniacal laugh. "YOU'RE IN!" he declared again, but much louder. "That's funny! Oh, you don't know HOW funny—but it's funny!" I'm not sure why, but I laughed and bid them all good night.

You're in?

How Slappy Became Cap'n

I was sleepin' below when Wee Johnny Weedsmoker burst in, shoutin', "He's goin' to blow us all up, Slappy!" I rolled out of my hammock, because this was somethin' I just had to see for meself.

Sure enough, Cap'n MacTavish was dancin' around a powder keg into which he had inserted a long, slow-burnin' fuse that he had just lit. He was singin' "Blow the Man Down" but instead o' "man" he sang "men" and instead o' "down" he sang "up."

While the rest o' the men pleaded with the madman, I quickly ordered the crew to toss the keg overboard. Sadly, when they made their move, Angus quickly lashed his body to the keg and secured himself with his MacTavish Knot o' Mystery. When the lads looked at me with that "what shall we do?" look, I returned it with a look and a nod o' me own, and over he went.

As we put a distance between ourselves and Cap'n MacTavish, we could hear him continue his singin'—except he was back to "man" from "men." After the spectacular explosion to our stern,

Cementhands McCormack slapped me on the back and said, "Well, Cap'n Slappy, where to now?"

What's in a Name? Ol' Chumbucket

Ol' Chumbucket is a mysterious figure aboard the ship. He holds no rank and his seamanship is spotty. He claims to have sailed on various other ships with various other pirate captains, except the dates don't seem to add up. Still, he exercises a surprising amount of authority aboard the ship as a result of his role as Cap'n Slappy's drinkin' buddy.

His name is also something of a mystery. As he tells it, "In 1717 I shipped out with Black Sam Bellamy aboard the *Whydah* as ship's cook. It's not easy to feed 144 picky pirates. The first night out I made my specialty, Flaming Seafood Surprise. The crew seemed unappreciative, tossing their bowls aside and threatening me with the cutlery. 'Look,' I said sternly, 'if ya don't eat it for dinner I'll serve it for breakfast.' And I did. And lunch, and dinner the next night. After a few days I kept to my cabin most of the time, and a good thing, because it took 'em a while to break down the door. They had just finished applying the tar when a howling nor'easter came up off Cape Cod. The ship went down with all hands and the treasure, but my protective coating of tar and feathers allowed me to swim ashore. I got nothin' for it but the nickname they gave me in appreciation of my cooking skills."

Other Hands on Board

The *Festering Boil* sails with a full complement of crew and officers. Many of them have names very similar to those of actual, living friends of ours, so we just want to make it clear that these are fictional characters, and we're not really calling any of our friends stupid or cranky or oddly obsessed with discipline. Heck no. We wouldn't do that to our friends. Would we? So they can just forget about calling those lawyers.

Jezebel the Web Wench, ship's engineering officer—A strange thing to have on board a seventeenth-century pirate ship, but a handy one. A science fiction fan who regards *Babylon 5* as the height of achievement, Jezebel maintains our Web site, which in the parlance of a pirate ship makes her the one who repairs the web of rigging should storm or enemy shot bring down a mast or spar. Jezebel was educated at the Edinburgh School of Knitting and Web Design. When the sails are straining, the lines pulled taut to the breaking point, it is always Jezebel who calls out in a thick Scottish accent, "She can't take much more, Cap'n!"

Mad Sally, official lusty pirate wench—Along with Jezebel, the insatiable Mad Sally is part of the real brain trust aboard the *Festering Boil*.

Francis Drake
Status: Privateer, not pirate
Feelings toward King Philip of Spain: Hated, hated, hated him, and any other Spaniard or papist
A privateer before becoming Elizabeth's chief admiral, Drake was the most resolute, domineering and amazing figure in the history of the sea. After one particularly successful raid down the Spanish Main, Drake took his ship, the *Golden Hind*, around the tip of South America and up the Pacific coast at least as far north as San Francisco. He was loath to retrace his route, believing the Spanish would be lying in wait for him, so he headed out across the uncharted Pacific, finally making it back by to England almost three years after departing, bringing tales of amazing adventures and an enormous treasure in loot. Drake was knighted by Queen Elizabeth for his exploits. Drake is the image of the dauntless sea dog.

Slappy and Ol' Chumbucket have lots of wild, funny ideas. Sally and Jez are the pair who keep things in order and make them run, discarding the guys' odder ideas without ever telling them about it. In that regard, Mad Sally serves as bos'n, the petty officer who actually runs the ship. She exercises a degree of control over the officers, particularly Ol' Chumbucket, which makes her the deciding voice in many a palaver. Mad Sally says she came from genteel stock, the daughter of a landed nobleman, but fled the stultifying life of society for the thrill of adventure on the high seas. That might even be true, although doubters point to her lack of even rudimentary understanding of table settings and the fact that a certain dockside doxie disappeared about the same time Sally first signed aboard.

Sawbones Burgess, ship's surgeon—Doc Burgess saved Cap'n Slappy's life one night when he unwisely picked a bar fight with the Spanish navy. The ENTIRE Spanish navy. As the fight progressed and fortune ceased to smile on Slappy in the battle, the good doctor took pity on him and mixed up a concoction of powder that he added to the rum that he offered to the enraged Spaniards. "Long live Queen Isabella!" he declared in perfect Spanish, and quickly passed the drinks out among the combatants—including Slappy. Finally, when everyone had a drink, he repeated his toast: "Long live Queen Isabella!" To which the crowd, including Slappy, responded, "Long live Queen Isabella!" and took a drink. Suddenly, they were all overcome with a sense of goodwill and a fascination for the way light seems all bouncy when it comes from a lantern. A Spanish captain observed, "But Queen Isabella, she's been dead for more than two hundred years!" But nobody cared and they slept off the rest of the night in a puppy pile. Slappy, who seemed unaffected by the drugged drink, hired Sawbones as ship's surgeon and master mixologist.

Lieutenant (pronounced LEF-tenant) Keeling, ship's disciplinarian and morale officer— The affable tenor and torture specialist was discovered by Cap'n Slappy during the 142nd Annual Pirate Olympics and Women's Beach Volleyball Extravaganza in Sao Paulo, Brazil. Keeling was the overall gold medalist in the Compulsory Multi-implement Flogging and Flaying Exercise and broke world and pirate records in all of the Cat categories as well as most of the standard keelhauling events. He enjoys gardening, long walks on the beach and Broadway musical theater. And despite his insatiable bloodlust and harsh disciplinary practices, he admits with a bit of a blush in his cheeks that he's a cuddler. Like THAT was a secret!

Able seaman Cementhands McCormack— He's a lovable giant of a man but not very bright. Some say he's got the strength of ten men and the brains of an after-dinner mint. And it's true that in battle, he's a raging monster of death, but he needs someone standing alongside to remind him not to pick up his own crewmates and toss them overboard. He once attacked and defeated a French fort wearing nothing but his kilt and armed only with a grapefruit spoon. Still, in his quiet and private moments he writes beautiful poetry about flowers in Sanskrit and once composed an opera about the life of Homer, called *Trojan Man*.

Dogwatch Watts—Once called Wrong Way Watts after a bold attempt to navigate the Amazon that ended up in Lake Michigan, Dogwatch nowadays can be found swinging the lead when passing over dangerous shoals, since he's the only crewman who can count to ten, as the others are all missing at least a couple of fingers. Also a good hand on lookout, as his eagle eye can spot a sail on the horizon even when it's just wishful thinking. A three-time winner and twice runner-up of *Tigerbeat Magazine*'s Cutest Pirate Contest.

QUICK QUIZ

1. A pirate's life was:
    a) weeks of dull routine periodically punctuated by a few hours of sheer terror
    b) for me
    c) taking the good with the bad, still more interesting than a college economics class
    d) a good excuse for a party
2. Blackbeard and his crew seem to have depended on their alcoholic beverages a bit too much. Can you think of anyone else of whom this is true? What about your wife's Uncle Dave?
3. Fill in the blank: If I were captain of a pirate ship, I'd keep my crew amused by ________.
4. How likely is it that Ol' Chumbucket really

served on the *Whydah,* considering that it sank in 1717 and he is alive and well as of this writing?

5. Do the friends of Cap'n Slappy and Ol' Chumbucket have grounds for a defamation lawsuit, or can the Pirate Guys fall back on the "all in good fun" defense?

20

It's Not Just a Job—It's Work!

In Which the aspiring pirate can apply for a position aboard the *Festering Boil*, and become part of our nautical fantasy life.

The Festering Boil
(An Equal Opportunity Destroyer)

APPLICATION FOR EMPLOYMENT

Thank you for your interest in employment aboard the world-famous pirate ship, the Festering Boil. *Filling out this application may be the first step in a life filled with adventure and excitement. Please answer honestly with the utmost transparency. We are not only looking for the best possible applicants, but we want to make sure that we are a good "fit" for you as well.*

1. Name: ____________________ ______________________________
   (given) (pirate—include modifiers)

2. Age:________ 3. Real Age:________ 4. Estimated Age:________

5. Seeking: full time (extended cruise) / part time (day raid) employment (circle one)

6. List any disabilities (e.g., missing limbs, eyes, ears, etc.) and modifications/adaptive apparatus (e.g., hooks, pegs, patches, ear horns, etc.)

   ____
   ____
   ____
   ____

Please note: Although having more than one disability and stereotypical adaptive apparatus is desirable, please don't list "missing toe" as "missing leg." It just doesn't count.

7. Have you ever been convicted of a felony? Yes/No (circle one)
If "No," explain why not. ______________________
If "Yes" please list felony convictions and subsequent punishments. Also list jurisdiction offense took place in, convicting court and references (defense attorney, parole officer, etc.).
____
____
____
____
(Use back of form if necessary.)

8. Are you a woman disguised as a man to stow away on a pirate ship for adventure? Yes/No
(circle one)
Please note: A "Yes" answer does not necessarily eliminate you from consideration. It simply allows Cap'n Slappy to get cleaned up for your interview.

9. Be honest. You ARE a woman, aren't you? Alright, you got me!/I said "No," ye drunken bastard!
(circle one) *(Fine! Have it your way! But you DO have a pretty mouth.)*

10. Please list in order, from one to four ("one" being "most willing"), the things you would be willing to do as a member of the *Festering Boil*'s crew.
____ a. Feed a French sailor's intestines to the ship's goat slowly, a few inches at a time, while he begs for a merciful death.
____ b. Host a Princess House Crystal party at your home and invite at least ten of your wealthiest friends, while they beg for a merciful death.
____ c. Use a missionary's fishing boat for cannon practice.
____ d. Sell life insurance to family members.

11. Life aboard a pirate ship is cramped and space for sleeping is limited. Which description best fits your personal sleep style? Spooner/Cuddler (circle one)

12. Please complete the following sentence choosing the option below that best fits your philosophy. *"I have always found that the best way to resolve a conflict between myself and a co-worker is to ______________________."*

    a. administer a savage beating with my fists and forehead
    b. remove all distractions and just talk, face-to-face, like "people"
    c. kill my co-worker and feed his body to some sort of carnivorous animal
    d. hire someone else to kill my co-worker and feed his body to some sort of carnivorous animal; then kill the person I hired and feed his body to that same carnivorous animal; then kill and eat that carnivorous animal

13. Please use the space provided to describe your pirate experience. Be sure to include any employment in the legal, insurance and public relations fields.

    ____

    ____

    ____

14. What do your birth signs (both the Piradiac and Pirate Year) tell us about your personality? Why should we hire you in spite of all of that?

    ____

    ____

    ____

15. In your lust for power and control due to your overwhelming ambition, please list, from one to four ("one" being "most willing"),

what you would be willing to do to take command of the *Festering Boil.*

____ a. I will bide my time and wait for the effects of Cap'n Slappy's chronic debauchery to consume him, then step in to fill the void.

____ b. I would launch a smear campaign in the media (the ship's log) and make Cap'n Slappy look like a flip-flopper who has used special favors over the years through family connections to gain and maintain power and, just to be sure, manipulate the voting process in order to defeat him during the elections. I would follow it up with a victory speech that acknowledges and thanks him for his years of dedicated service and contributions to worldwide piracy.

____ c. I would kill him in his sleep.

____ d. I would hire someone to kill him in his sleep and feed him to a carnivorous animal. Then I would kill the person I hired and feed him to that same carnivorous animal. Then I would kill the carnivorous animal in question and eat it.

Please read and sign the following:

I hereby assert that the above represents exactly what I want it to represent and that anything else is none of your damn business. Please note that I am not scared of anyone in your damn crew with the exception of Cementhands McCormack but only because of his massive size and general twitchiness. If you are smart enough to hire me, I will do what I want, say what I want and if you don't like it, then we got us a problem, don't we? That's about it. I look forward to working with you.

______________________________ ______________________________

(signature or X) *(date or XXV)*

Notarized by: ______________________________

Pursuant to Pirate Code 34/s-17.3, the above information is considered confidential unless otherwise specified or found to be useful for extortion/blackmail purposes. Cap'n Slappy and the Board of Directors of the *Festering Boil* retain the right to refuse employment based on nothing more than whimsy and alcohol-induced hallucinations.

Thank you for your application.

21

Therapist's Notes from Pirate Group Sessions

Several years ago, Dr. Cyrus Papoulopogas—noted psychiatrist and author of the books *Sad Pirate/Happy Pirate* and *What Color is Your Treasure Chest?*—worked with a small group of notable pirates in an effort to bring them some level of comfort and peace. The following are excerpts from his notebook which was found in the men's restroom of Mad Sally's Whistle Wetter in Pompano Beach, Florida.

June 11, 1978—Our first session. In attendance are Edward "Blackbeard" Teach, William Kidd, Sir Francis Drake, Henry Morgan, Bartholomew Roberts, Calico Jack Rackham, Stede Bonnet, Mark Read and Jean Laffite. I am always a bit leery of court-mandated counseling. If a person has to be ordered to counseling, that's just another roadblock, and these people definitely don't seem to want to be here. I have tried to make them feel at home, but the fact that I am in a room with nine heavily armed, ill-tempered pirates (some of the notorious variety) is more than a little off-putting. (Note to self: Avoid using words like "off-putting.") I decided to clear the air and, as an exercise of trust, confess my fearful feelings to the group. This had an undesired effect on the group that took the form of jokes at my expense—mostly of the "urinating on myself" variety. (Note to self: Avoid confessing fearful feelings to the group.)

Edward Teach insists on being called Blackbeard and emphasized his point by twisting fuses into his beard and lighting them on fire. (Pyromania?) The smallest of the pirates, Mark Read, seems to be overcompensating via numerous attempts to spit and thwack his small, shapely thigh. Several of the pirates, Henry Morgan most aggressively, seemed strangely drawn to the young man. (Latent homosexuality rampant amongst seafaring men?) Stede Bonnet tried to sit

Errol Flynn
Status: Actor
Success with women: Legendary
In *Captain Blood* and again in *The Sea Hawk* (they were virtually the same movie; they even used some of the same footage), Errol Flynn was probably the greatest cinema pirate ever. In fact, forget the probably. He was. He played pirates in movies that had nothing to do with pirates and were shot in the desert. He just had that way—the smile, the bounce, the pirattitude. Now, somewhere out there someone is spitting his warm milk and saying, "Wait, in those movies he was a privateer, not a pirate." But that's neither here nor there. The point is, Errol Flynn was the man. He was it.

close to Read, but quickly moved away when William Kidd swung a bucket at his head. Bartholomew Roberts finally threw young Mr. Read's chair aside and made him sit on his lap and perform a ventriloquist show. (Personality displacement?)

During introductions, nobody was willing or able to answer the "If you were a tree, what kind of tree would you be?" self-diagnostic question, although Jean Laffite did suggest that Stede Bonnet would be a weeping willow, which brought an explosion of laughter from the group (excluding Bonnet, of course). Group structure broke down immediately.

The session ended in gunfire and swordplay. No one was killed, but there was a remarkable amount of blood on the floor. (Note to self: Send the cleaning bill to the court.)

June 18, 1978—I can see that Edward "Blackbeard" Teach is going to be a real challenge. He is clearly a rage-aholic and suffers from a marked detachment from reality. (Well, I am not sure how much HE suffers from it, but everyone around him does.) Try as I might, I was unable to convince him to put words to his outbursts or in any way make an "I" statement about his feelings (e.g., "I feel sad when you criticize my choice of weapon").

There may be a thicker layer of latent homosexuality present in this group than I expected. Calico Jack Rackham is the only member of the group that is currently living with his wife, who he suspects may have taken up a romantic relationship with another woman. Henry Morgan asked him to "describe what evidence ye have of such a carnal union between women—and spare us no detail, no matter how sordid!" Mark Read, perched happily on Sir Francis Drake's knee, seemed particularly intent. The entire group was on the edge of their chairs but Rackham declined to offer up any such details.

William Kidd kept looking around my office and digging holes in my floor with a pickax and shovel. (Extensive carpet damage—to be billed to the court.) Sir Francis Drake insisted that he was late for an audience with the queen and if he didn't get going he would "lose his head." I used this as an opportunity to interject a few words on emotional control and personal responsibility. "Nobody," I said, "is going to 'lose his head' if he is late for a meeting—we are here to gain the skills necessary to keep our heads on straight." Blackbeard quickly discounted my "teachable moment" through thunderous laughter.

The session erupted in gunfire and swordplay. Stede Bonnet made an attempt to play peacemaker, but he was knocked unconscious by William Kidd and his deadly chum-bucket.

June 25, 1978—Edward "Blackbeard" Teach is making good progress. He confronted Calico

Jack Rackham about the fact that he is keeping his wife, Anne Bonney, at an emotional distance. Jack was able to acknowledge Edward's observation, but couldn't resist pointing out that the fiery wicks in Edward's beard could also be construed as intentionally uninviting. And William Kidd kept scratching his eyebrow with his middle finger and chortling to himself. Bartholomew Roberts and Mark Read didn't even go through the motions of group process today. They simply sat on the couch and took turns tickling each other.

Moments later, the session ended in gunfire and swordplay. Rackham took cover in the coat closet.

July 2, 1978—William Kidd continues in denial. "I don't belong here. I'm not a pirate!" he said. Sir Francis Drake is starting to join him in the assertion, claiming that a privateer is a patriot! Edward "Blackbeard" Teach keeps muttering that they "ought to get a room." It's all I can do to keep order when they get on this topic. Finally, Jean Laffite resolved the issue by declaring that "one man's privateer is another man's pirate!" Kidd came unglued and lunged at Laffite from the other side of the circle, screaming, "Ye stinkin' frog!" at which point Bartholomew Roberts stunned Kidd with a sharp blow from a belaying pin he had in his coat pocket. Kidd returned to his chair, rubbing his head. When I confronted Roberts about bringing a weapon to group, he simply pointed out that "a be-layin' pin is for keepin' things secure—and that's what I was doin'." Mark Read quickly checked Kidd for injuries and offered to "kiss the boo-boo." Everyone watched while he did. (Note to self: Double-check Mr. Read's medical history. Is there anything in there about man-breast augmentation surgery?)

Moments later, the session ended in gunfire and swordplay. Henry Morgan chased Stede Bonnet around the room spanking him with his sword.

July 9, 1978—(First session after my "No Firearms, Blunt Instruments or Sharp Objects" memo went out to the group.) Today's theme: "Reality is a Harsh Mistress." Stede Bonnet started group on a very dark tone during our "check-in" time. He made the point that with the possible exception of me (the therapist), the members of the group had two things in common:

They are all pirates.

They have all been dead for over two hundred years.

This, Jack Rackham pointed out, was a "downer." And the group voted immediately to have Stede "keelhauled." I intervened by insisting that, if someone was going to be keelhauled for expressing himself, the therapeutic process would be severely retarded. Just as I was about to rephrase my observation, Edward Teach pulled out a pistol, aimed it in my direction and bellowed, "Now we'll just SEE who's retarded!" and fired.

Needless to say, I was taken by surprise, but when the smoke from his flintlock pistol cleared, I realized that I had not been harmed at all. He had, in fact, shot Bonnet in the chest. Stede was stunned. I was stunned. I asked him if he was alright. "No!" he shouted, near tears. "He shot me in my fucking chest! How would you like it if he shot you in your fucking chest?" The best answer I could manage was, "Well, not very much, I suppose." His response was not much better: "Well, I didn't think so—and sorry about using the F word."

Francis Drake pointed out that the wound certainly wasn't going to kill Bonnet. "My dear boy," he said, "as you have taken great pains to remind all of us, you are already dead." Perhaps it was the obvious irony or maybe it was Sir Francis' kind fatherly tone, but this seemed to perk Stede up a bit—that coupled with the fact that Mark Read slinked over and straddled Bonnet's lap and in the sexiest little baby voice said, "Did somebody hurt mama's little boy?" and then started making out with him. Then he performed a striptease in the center of the group circle in which it became apparent to me (as it had always been apparent to the rest of the group) that "he" was in fact a "she."

Moments later, the session ended in the traditional swordplay and firearms display. Henry

Morgan had managed to smuggle a huge cannon in under his coat. (Note to self: Don't accept "codpiece" explanation anymore.)

July 16, 1978—Closing Group. Usually, when I close a group, I like to end with some finality ritual, but I found myself oddly drawn to this collection of rogues, ruffians and a cross-dressing nymphomaniac. I worked hard all week to find just the right costume and after some initial piratical chortling, I told them that they had inspired me—that I was now going to change careers and become a pirate. The chortling became a burst of laughter. Even Stede Bonnet mocked my life-changing intention. "You?! A pirate!?!" So I pulled out a pistol and shot him in the head. (I knew it wouldn't kill him—as has been established in previous group sessions—but it did make him whine and complain.) After the shot, the group exploded in thunderous laughter and applause.

"Well, me boy," Blackbeard declared with a clap on my back, "I do believe our work here is finished." And with that, the group got up to leave. "No! Wait! You are court-ordered to finish this hour!" Henry Morgan wheeled around and drew his pistol. Leveling it at my head he said, "No, lad. YOU'RE Court-ordered to finish this hour. And that's Court with a capital C. Ye see, ye've been operating under the misguided impression that We're the only ones in this group who are dead."

I sat back down, stunned. Jean Laffite picked up the explanation. "You see, mon ami, the Judge—and that's with a capital J—was putting you through your purgatorial paces and we are your final test—to do therapy with the eternally incorrigible. You've passed, mon ami, congratulations." Mary Read sauntered across the room and kissed me gently but deeply on the mouth. "You are SO cute!" She turned and walked out the door with the rest.

As Bartholomew Roberts was closing the door behind them I called out, "But I don't want to go to heaven! I want to go with you!" He paused in the doorway and smiled. "What exactly do you think 'heaven' is, boy?"

I'd like to thank the Court for this opportunity. I've never had so little control over something or felt so lost. Perhaps that was the point the Judge was trying to make. But as I look out my office window into a harbor that was never there before, I see a ship waiting. After so many years of writing in pirate metaphor but living life close to the vest, I now have a chance to take that great adventure and this time, I won't miss the boat.

Respectfully Submitted for Approval,

The Better Late Than Never Cyrus Papoulopogas, PhD

P.S. Please don't leave these notes in the men's restroom of Mad Sally's Whistle Wetter like you did with my notebook on that Russian Cossack group I did last year.

The official scoring guide for the Pi-Q will be found in your own backyard. (As Dorothy told the Scarecrow—it was there all along!)

Just remove this "X" from the book (or copy it onto a piece of paper) and place it randomly in your backyard or nearby public park. Then dig a three-feet-deep hole under the spot that "X" marks, and you will find the answer to your Piratical Quotient.

Trust us on this. If you don't find it on the first dig, try again. Keep track of the number of times you dig a hole looking for the answers. Multiply that number by ten and subtract it from one hundred. THAT is your Pi-Q!

(If you don't dig any holes, your score is 100—that, of course, makes you average and uninteresting.)

(If you dig a hole and in fact find buried treasure instead of the answers, give yourself an added thirty points and contact the authors immediately to inform them of their 50 percent share in the treasure. It's only fair. You wouldn't be digging at all if it weren't for our "X," now, would you?)

Acknowledgments

All along the path of this amazing adventure there have been family, friends, strangers and enthusiastic supporters helping us out and cheering us on. At the risk of forgetting someone who deserves recognition (and we're pretty disorganized, so it's sure to happen), we'd like to thank some of the people who gave so willingly of their time and their energy for us.

None of this would have happened if Dave Barry hadn't responded to our cockamamie e-mail. He keeps trying to duck any credit, but we know we wouldn't have gotten anywhere without his boost. Thanks, Dave. We'll buy you a beer or two someday. And we'll buy another for Judi Smith, Dave's Research Department, who has helped and supported us all along the way.

We've had tons of help from a host of people in the pirate enthusiast community (a surprisingly huge community!). We won't be able to thank even a fraction of the people we should, but we have to give a shout-out to Christine "Jamaica Rose" Lampe of *No Quarter Given*. She's an invaluable source of information when you want to know something accurate, which, surprisingly, we did from time to time. If she doesn't know the answer, she knows who does. Thanks to pirate artist Don Maitz, a splendid painter, and special thanks to Mark Jensen and all of the Seattle Seafair Pirates—mad men with swords!

We have sometimes wondered, when watching awards shows on television, why winners thanked their agents—it always seemed crass to us. Now we understand. Your agent is the first person outside your immediate family to believe in you, and sometimes even your family has doubts. Scott Hoffman at PMA Literary and Film Management believed in us longer than he reasonably could have been expected to, and made this book happen. Thanks, Scott. Even then he might not have succeeded had he not hooked us up with Liz Scheier, our incredibly positive and almost frighteningly supportive editor at New American Library.

A special word to copy editor Cherilyn Johnson: We're sorry. This couldn't have been at all straightforward or easy, and you did a splendid job. Any errors that remain are due to our pigheadedness.

Our whole pirate journey has been like yearlong summer camp to a couple of kids. Thanks to the grown-ups who keep us steady, attorney Tom Black, accountant Nick Cutting and talent agent Lynne Theisen of Big Fish NW. Also thanks to Dr. Tom Costello, Bennett Hall, the marvelous singer-songwriter Tom Smith and Ardie Flynn of Flappin' Flags in Eugene. And special thanks to Jeff Boatwright and Gene and Susan Gregg: Thanks for the beer.

To our many, many friends, especially the extended family at Albany Civic Theater, thank you all. Special thanks to George Lauris, Oscar B. Hult, Stephanie Long, Robyn Oslon, Reid and Angela Byers, Brian Rhodes, Sandy McCormack, Gregg Burgess, Paul and Kris Watts, Dean and Mirinda (Red Molly) Keeling, Jan and Jim Donnelly, Christi Sears, Leonora Rianda, Anya Corbitt, Julia Morizawa, Alan Nessett, Dan and Harriet Nixon, Don Taco, Robert Leff and Gary Tharp, and the dozens we've forgotten to mention here. Your friendship is precious to us.

To Pat Kight, the Web Wench, who has donated so much time and energy to making us look like we're something out on the Web. You're a miracle worker, Pat.

And finally, to our families.

To Tori, the Official Lusty Pirate Wench and a woman without whom not a word of this book would have been written. You are the perfect pirate's partner and Ol' Chumbucket is madly in love with you. To the Baur kids—Jack, Alex, Ben, Kate, Millie and Max—thanks for not dying of embarrassment over this whole pirate thing. To Janet "Leaky Pump" Hiltabidel, thanks for everything.

To Mark's ex-wife, Rhonda, who showed her remarkable sense of humor and graciousness in sharing her birthday with all the pirates of the world, we offer thanks and apologies. Thanks as well to Mark's parents and brothers, who showed that laughter at the dinner table could prevent violence in the rumpus room.

Photo by Karl Maasdam, Karl Maasdam Photography

They didn't have a dream, not even a plan. It was more of a whimsical notion. But it was enough to take them from a YMCA racquetball court to stage, radio, television and newspaper appearances around the world, and a staggering nineteen million hits on their Web site in just one month. They are **Mark "Cap'n Slappy" Summers** and **John "Ol' Chumbucket" Baur**, two friends from Oregon who created International Talk Like a Pirate Day and took the idea way too far.

Mark was born and grew up in Seattle, the fourth of five brothers. His maritime background includes his father, who was an engineer on Boeing's Marine System Division working on projects such as the jet foil, and his grandfather and uncles, fishermen on Washington's coast. Mark earned a master's degree in social work at Portland State University and works as a school social worker. He really should know better than this, but here he is.

John hails from Chicago, where he was the only son among eight kids. After earning a bachelor's degree in political science, John worked in the daily newspaper business, practicing what one humorless editor called "smart-ass journalism." He then worked two years as a science writer before stumbling into this racket.

It was during a racquetball game several years ago, when they both still labored under the delusion that they could stay in shape, that they came up with the idea for Talk Like a Pirate Day. They chose September 19 because it was Summers' ex-wife's birthday. As he said, "The date was stuck in my brain and I wasn't doing anything with it anymore." From such an unlikely beginning, an international event was born.

So Mark is famously divorced, and lives alone in a house in which he experiments painting the walls unusual colors. John is married to Tori, the Official Lusty Pirate Wench. Together they have what their friends refer to as "many, many children." Mark and John continue to fantasize that they can somehow turn this pirate thing into a paying gig and never have to have a real job again.